Jui

C000186600

THE INEVITABLE END

They shook hands like comrades. For the
second time since he had known her, he
drew confidence from that firm, boyish clasp
of her fingers. She, looking up at him, scoffed
at the memory of Lady Jo's cynical outlook
upon her engagement.

'One of these days your steely young man
will lose his head and kiss you – then the fat
will be in the fire!,' had been one of Jo's
remarks. Billie regarded her fiancé's face,
strong, dogged, rather splendid in the
starlight, and smiled to herself. Richard was
not the sort to lose his head. For an instant
she imagined such a situation – Richard
seizing her in his arms; that stern firm mouth
closing upon her own...

A thrill of acute terror and dismay darted
through her heart. She hastily muttered
another good-night, and fled into the Club.
Her cheeks were flame-colour, like her cloak.

'Heavens! I should hate him like poison if
he ever did such an outrageous thing,' she
told herself furiously.

**Also by the same author,
and available in Coronet Books:**

The Boundary Line
Come Back Yesterday
The Cyprus Love Affair
Forbidden
For The Sake Of Love
House Of The Seventh Cross
Laurence My Love
Life's A Game
The Other Side Of Love
Restless Heart
The Strong Heart
Sweet Cassandra
Twice Have I Loved
Unlit Fire
We Two Together
Stranger Than Fiction (Autobiography)
The Marriage Bond
A Promise Is For Ever
Brief Ecstasy
Slave Woman
To Love Again
White Jade
Sweet Love

The Inevitable End

Denise Robins

CORONET BOOKS
Hodder and Stoughton

Copyright © Denis Robins

First published in Great Britain in 1927 by
Mills and Boon

Coronet edition 1986

British Library C.I.P.

Robins, Denise
  The inevitable end
  1. Title
  823'.912[f]   PR6035.0554

  ISBN 0-340-39457-9

Printed and bound in Great Britain for
Hodder and Stoughton Paperbacks, a
division of Hodder and Stoughton Ltd.,
Mill Road, Dunton Green, Sevenoaks,
Kent (Editorial Office: 47 Bedford
Square, London, WC1 3DP) by
Hunt Barnard Ltd., Aylesbury, Bucks.

CHAPTER 1

IT was between Storrington and Parham that the big blue car with the gleaming silver bonnet, which had been travelling through Sussex at breakneck speed, leaving a cloud of dust behind it, suddenly broke down.

The girl at the wheel drew up, and jumped out.

'Water in the carburettor,' she muttered. 'Dash the thing!'

She drew off her gauntlets, and lifted up the bonnet of the car.

After tinkering with the carburettor for a moment, she drew back, wiped her forehead with the back of a small oil-stained hand, and took off her felt hat, which she threw into the car with a vicious little movement.

'Botheration!' she said aloud. 'I believe it's something more than water in the thing ... it *would* happen just as I'm so near home ... and a thunder-storm coming up, too!'

She pulled a slim gold case out of her pocket, and lit a cigarette. Frowning, she looked up at the sky. It had been a matchless blue all this exquisite May day. But now the clouds were gathering, and across the commons and the woods dark shadows crept, where a few moments before the sunlight had been streaming goldenly.

Over Chanctonbury Ring the sky was ominously streaked with orange. Not a breath of wind stirred the leaves. There was that close silence which heralds a storm.

The girl stood by the side of the car, smoking for a moment. Then she looked up at the sky again.

'Now for a storm,' she muttered.

The hood and side-curtains were easily manipulated. She

5

put them up just in time. Down came the rain—big, heavy drops—accompanied by a low growl of thunder.

The girl looked at her wristlet watch, and saw that it was a quarter-past four..

'I wired Vera that I'd be home for tea ...' she reflected. 'But it doesn't look as though I shall have any tea to-day. If I were on the main road, I'd be able to get help. Can't think why I chose this by-road to break down on!'

The rain fell faster, and the first vivid flash of lightning illuminated the hills. The girl climbed into her car with a sigh of resignation, prepared to remain therein until help arrived. The storm did not affect her. She lit another cigarette, and watched the lightning play over Chanctonbury and the gorse-covered common.

She remained like this for ten minutes. Then she sat up and threw away her cigarette. A man was coming down the road, striding through the rain with lowered head. He wore grey flannels and an old tweed coat, and his head was bare. He was walking very fast.

The girl hailed him.

'Most males understand cars,' she thought. 'I hope to goodness this one does. Hi! hi!' she called, waving her hand.

The man looked up and approached the car.

'Hullo! Anything wrong?' he called back.

'No—that's why I'm sitting here listening to the thunder,' she said, with biting sarcasm.

He reached the car and stared at her.

'Well— what is the matter?' he asked huffily.

'Car won't go,' she said. 'Do you know anything about it?'

'A bit,' he said. 'I'll look, if you like.'

'Well, you seem pretty wet already, so it won't go to my heart to see you get a bit wetter,' she said.

He stared at her again. Her abrupt manner seemed to surprise him, and he thought her rather rude. She was quite young; the slim figure in the tailormade suit and suede motoring-coat was immature and boyish. She looked about nineteen. Her whole appearance was boyish rather than

6

womanly. Her hair—light brown—was cut short and waved naturally back from her forehead. She had sharp features, and a clear, sun-browned skin. Her shirt-blouse, open at the neck, showed a V of tanned throat. Even the eyes were the eyes of a boy—grey-green, and very keen, with short black lashes.

He turned from her, after a brief scrutiny, and began to examine the engine. Every now and then he shook his head, and wiped the raindrops from his face. The lightning continued to flash vividly, and the thunder rolled magnificently and with increasing power, over the hills.

The girl had stepped into the road, and was standing unconcernedly in the rain, watching the man make his examination. She had given him one cursory glance, and summed him up in a few words:

'Sahib from his voice ... no money from his clothes; and too good-looking ... bound to be a conceited prig ... however, useful at the moment ...'

He looked up at her.

'Puncture in the float,' he said. 'You won't be able to get on. She'll have to be towed to the nearest garage.'

'That's pleasant,' said the girl crossly. 'What a beastly nuisance! And how am I going to get home?'

'Do you live far away?'

'Just outside Brighton.'

'You could hire a car from a garage in Storrington.'

'Yes, I could do that.'

'Well, I've got an ancient motor-bike, and I could get you into Storrington on that, when the storm subsides.'

'Thanks,' she said. 'That's decent of you.'

'Meanwhile,' he said, 'you'd better shelter back at my place. This is rather a nasty storm.'

'Where do you live?'

'That cottage—over there ...' he pointed to the only dwelling visible on the landscape—a small white-washed cottage with a thatched roof and diamond-paned windows. The girl followed his gaze, then looked at him doubtfully.

7

Good-looking he certainly was; tall and broad-shouldered, with the narrow hips that women appraise. His features were straight, and he had a clear, bronzed skin, and thick dark hair with an attractive 'kink' in it. But the expression of his mouth was surly, and his eyes—very blue—were the most cynical, bitter eyes she had ever seen. Eager invitation and admiration from him would have made her at once refuse to shelter in his cottage. But the fact that this invitation was merely the outcome of breeding and courtesy, and uttered none too graciously, found favour with her.

'I dare say you'd like a cup of tea,' he added. 'There's nobody at home but the woman who looks after the place, and my young brother.'

The girl jammed her hat down on her head.

'Right-o,' she said. 'I'll come. And thanks.'

She fell into step beside him, and began to walk across the sodden field toward the little cottage.

'Under the circumstances we might as well know each other's names,' she said, after a pause. 'Mine is Billie Carden.'

'It would be "Billie",' he thought. 'She looks like it. One of these young women of the new masculine cult!' Aloud he said: 'My name's Bromley—Richard Bromley.'

'You've chosen a solitary spot to live in,' she remarked.

A loud crackle of thunder downed his reply, but he repeated it:

'I don't live in this place by choice, I assure you. I'd be abroad if I had the chance. But I've got no money, and a delicate brother to look after, so I live in the cheapest way possible.'

'I see,' said Billie. 'You don't do any work, then?'

'Work!' He gave a short laugh. 'My work consists of writing stories and selling 'em when I can—and digging the garden in my spare time.'

'Well, it might be worse,' said Billie thoughtfully. 'You're lucky to be able to sell your stories at all.'

'Quite so,' he said, with another laugh.

'What do you write? The usual love-rot?'

'Heaven forbid!' he said. 'I keep strictly to adventure. I couldn't write a line on love. I don't believe in it.'

'I'm with you there,' she said, flashing a more friendly look at him. 'Neither do I believe in it. What is love? A snare and a delusion. I've never wanted any romance or sentiment in my life, and I don't intend to have it. I've seen too many of my girl-pals mess up their lives with love.'

Richard Bromley nodded.

'Yes, mess up their lives, and the lives of the unfortunate men they set themselves out to capture,' he said grimly.

'Oh, it's six of one and half a dozen of the other,' said Billie. 'Men are selfish brutes. They turn women into fools, then go about calling them fools. But no man will ever be able to call *me* one! I make them keep their distance. I don't mind a decent man-pal—but a lover—pah! The mere idea makes me feel sick!'

Bromley shook with silent laughter.

'You're a queer sort of girl,' he said. 'You've cut out the "soft-stuff," have you? So have I. But I've had rotten experiences, and you, apparently, have had none.'

'Don't want any,' said Billie calmly.

'Don't be too sure,' he said. 'I've met your sort before—the woman who swears she has no use for my sex, and ends up by coming a howler with some cad or other.'

'Not me,' said Billie grimly. 'I've got my head screwed on the right way.'

'Some women are driven to marriage—for the sake of a home and money.'

'There, again, I escape. I'm fortunate enough to possess a private income.'

He nodded his head, regarding her without much interest.

'You're certainly lucky. Well, here we are. You'd better go in and get dry by the kitchen fire.'

Later, when Billie was tolerably dry, she found her way into the sitting-room; and a tempting tea with hot buttered toast and home-made scones was placed before her.

CHAPTER 2

RICHARD BROMLEY joined Billie. He had been out in the shed to inspect his motorcycle, and then up to his room to change into another suit—which Billie noticed was only a shade less shabby than the first one he had worn.

'The storm's passing over,' he announced. 'My bike's all right. We'll be able to get to Storrington after tea, and tell them at the garage to send for your little bus.'

'Thanks awfully,' said Billie. 'Can I give you some tea, or would you rather pour it out?'

'I'd rather pour it out myself,' he said.

He spoke rather bluntly. He was so used to being without a woman in the house: he felt he did not want one 'to look after him' now. To see this girl pour out his tea would remind him too painfully of the old days (they seemed centuries ago!) when the woman he had loved desperately—and lost so desperately—had held this very teapot in her dainty hands, smiling at him with all her sex-allure, as she handed him the cup.

Billie Carden was not in the least like that woman, however. He was almost thankful for the lack of soft femininity about this unexpected guest. She was so like a boy with her severe blue tailor-made, white shirt-blouse, and short brown hair.

Tea over, they smoked and exchanged a few confidences.

Billie explained that she had been spending the weekend with a friend in Chichester. She had motored back this way, just for a whim. The weather had seemed so fine; there had been no need to hurry. She lived with a cousin—Miss Vera

Disney—in a bungalow which she had built on the Downs a few miles out of Brighton.

She was, apparently, a most fortunate and independent young woman: an orphan; no ties; no cares—heiress to an uncle who was an American millionaire. She was American on her father's side, but had lived all her life in England. She spent the spring and summer in England, and generally went abroad with her cousin in the winter.

Richard Bromley regarded her with an almost hostile look in his eyes.

'You're thoroughly spoiled,' he growled. 'What right have you to all the goods of this world, and no troubles?'

'The troubles of this life are either financial or sentimental,' said Billie. 'Since I am free from the former, I shall take care to keep free from the latter.'

'Very wise,' he said, with a short laugh. 'I've been the sort of fool to court both. But my chief trouble of the moment is my young brother, who is upstairs in bed, and has been in bed for months now. He's got spinal trouble, poor kid—only sixteen, too. He ought to be operated on—to have proper treatment, and I can't afford it. It's the very devil!'

'Rotten luck,' said Billie.

'Tony has nobody to look after him but me,' said Richard. 'I'm sixteen years older, and father died soon after he was born, so I've always been father as well as brother to Tony. Then, two years ago, the mater died, too. Tony and I were left alone. I was in a good position on the Stock Exchange. My partner let me down and absconded with all the money, leaving me to pay off huge liabilities. Of course it ruined me, and I had to give up the Exchange.'

'Bad luck all round,' murmured Billie. 'But a good thing you weren't married and with a large family.'

'I *was* married,' Richard said in a low voice. 'I was ... that's just it. Though I had no family, thank God ... only Tony to look after.'

Billie puffed at her cigarette in silence. Any display of weakness or emotion made her speechless. Entirely lacking

11

in sentiment herself, she did not understand or sympathise with it in others. Yet she was sorry in a vague way for this blue-eyed, good-looking giant, who had obviously been through the mill one way and another.

He continued to confide in her, as though it pleased him to pour out his bitterness, his virulence against her sex.

'My wife was very beautiful—the most charming creature in the world,' he said. 'I was a complete fool about her, and she pretended to be one about me ... possibly was ... for as long as it suited her. But when the crash came ... she couldn't face the poverty or my irritability ... and God knows I was irritable and bitter those days, after being let down so badly by my partner. Then she crowned everything by letting me down in a worse way.'

'Ran away?' put in Billie's cool voice.

'Yes ... with some fellow in the Guards who had more money than he needed and no scruples about taking her. So Tony and I had to fight things out by ourselves. I couldn't get a fresh job ... so we came down here, and I support the two of us by writing.'

'H'm,' said Billie. 'It's the same old story. What is love? You shouldn't have married.'

'Oh, some folk make a better job of marriage than I've done,' said Richard Bromley, with a curt laugh. 'All marriages don't end in divorce.'

'Most marriages are mistakes and ought to end in divorce,' said Billie, 'only in a good many cases the folk are too stupid (or too virtuous) to separate. To crave for divorce in one's mind, and not dare to take any action, is immoral to my way of thinking, so the most moral thing to do is to remain single.'

Richard Bromley pulled a pipe from his coat-pocket and handled the polished bowl with fingers that looked both strong and tender. But there was no tenderness on his face. He looked hard ... hard as nails ... and that was what Billie Carden appreciated most in him.

'He may have been a fool once, but he won't be a fool

twice,' she mentally decided. 'I think I like him.'

She was so sick of, and bored with, the many men she met who begged her to forsake the road of stern realism and tread the path of dreams. It was a novelty and a pleasure to come in contact with a man who had proved by personal experience just what she believed—that the road of dreams ends in an abyss of darkness and misery.

Before she left the cottage, she went upstairs to see the invalid brother. She found Tony Bromley the most pathetic person she had ever met. Small, delicate as a child, he was more like a beautiful girl than a lad of sixteen. He had Richard's thick dark hair ... only it was a mass of curls ... and Richard's straight features. But his eyes were violet-blue, and much too large for his thin, white face. He looked terribly ill and frail, and there were lines of pain pulling down his mouth.

He greeted Billie without enthusiasm. He did not care for women ... he bore her sex a grudge because of the way in which his brother had been treated. But Billie Carden was so frankly boyish and unaffected that she weakened his antagonism.

He complained peevishly to Richard of the heat, and the bad effect which the thunder-storm had had on his head. Billie wondered how Richard would take the complaint, and saw him as one transformed. He was marvellously gentle and understanding with his young brother.

'The storm's over and the air's much cooler, old chap,' he said, shaking up the boy's pillows. 'Try and get a nap. When I've taken Miss Carden into Storrington, I'll come back and read a bit to you.'

'Good-bye, Tony,' said Billie, smiling at him with her keen grey-green eyes. 'By the way, I've got a topping library at my bungalow, and if you're hard up for anything to read, I'll send you something over.'

Tony's eyes lit up.

'Thanks awfully,' he said.

'That'd be kind of you, Miss Carden,' said Richard.

'Oh, rot!' she said, in her slangy, breezy way.

Richard Bromley followed her downstairs and out into the garden.

The rain had ceased. The air was cool and sweet. A light breeze shook the raindrops from the trees on to the soaked grass. In the west, a shaft of sunlight had escaped from the clouds and was fringing Chanctonbury Ring with living gold.

On the pillion of an old motor-bike, lightly holding on to Richard Bromley, Billie Carden rode into Storrington.

CHAPTER 3

VERA DISNEY sat on the edge of her cousin's bed, and listened with rapt interest to the tale of the breakdown and the tea in the cottage on the road to Parham.

'It sounds most thrilling, my dear Billie,' she said. 'Richard Bromley is a man after my own heart. Six-foot odd; blue eyes; a cynical mouth; and has divorced his wife. What romance!'

Billie, who was standing before her dressing-table vigorously brushing her hair, hunched her slim shoulders.

'You make me sick, Vera,' she said in a disgusted voice. 'You see romance in everything. Preserve us from it! Haven't you lived with me long enough to know that I dislike anything approaching romance? You can have your Richard Bromley.'

'I wonder if you'll ever see him again, my dear.'

'Probably not— and I don't want to.'

Vera smiled a trifle pityingly at Billie's straight back. She had never understood her young cousin's point of view, and was inclined to be scornful of it. But she was always very sweet to her—Vera's bread and butter depended on Billie. But then, Vera was sweet to everybody. She was the antithesis of her cousin; essentially feminine; the kind of girl who adores frilly, silky lingerie and Paris creations. She was very pretty in a magazine-cover way; golden hair; big blue eyes; a complexion of strawberries and cream, and a tiny rosebud mouth. She was a strong, selfish, coldly calculating character, but she adopted an appealing 'baby' manner which deceived even Billie.

'Vera's a little stupid, but she means well, and she's a good person to live with because she doesn't argue with me, and doesn't mind how rude I am to her,' was Billie's private criticism of her cousin.

As a matter of fact, Vera was jealous of Billie; envied her money and independence most bitterly. But she was dependent on Billie for the good things of this life, and Billie was extraordinarily generous. It was worth while remaining with her and pandering to her whims.

Billie had just emerged from her bath. Her tanned face glowed with health and spirits. She had put on a severe blue frock, which suited her boyish style. Vera, as usual, was in a delicate foamy georgette gown—looking exquisite.

'You haven't read your letter from Uncle Silas, yet,' Vera reminded her cousin.

'Nor have I,' said Billie, picking up a fat letter with the U.S.A. postmark, which lay on her bed. 'Light me a cig, there's a dear, Vera.'

Vera obeyed. Every mail that came, she secretly hoped that Silas G. Carden might ask his niece and heiress to join him in New York. She was sick to death of the simple life on the Sussex Downs which Billie forced her to lead. What chance had she, Vera, of meeting a decent man with money, and marrying him—so long as Billie avoided people and devoted all her time to outdoor sport?

She handed Billie a lighted cigarette, but the girl did not take it. She was intent upon her letter. She read it to the end. Then she looked up at Vera. There was a queer, dismayed

15

look in her grey-green eyes, and Vera fancied she had lost some of her healthy colour.

'My dear—what's up?' Vera murmured.

'My God!' said Billie, in a blunt voice. 'This has done it.'

'What?'

'Uncle Silas has gone mad.'

'Gone mad! What do you mean?'

'Read it,' said Billie, thrusting the letter before her.

Vera read it. It was a long, neatly written epistle, couched in the usual frank, curt terms adopted by the Carden family. The gist of it was this. Silas G. Carden had decided that it was high time his niece and heiress took a husband. He knew her prejudices against marriage. He strongly disapproved of spinsters and the modern masculine type of woman who snaps her fingers at the male sex, and refused to take up the true woman's burden of matrimony and motherhood. It was not only his desire but *his command* that Billie should marry—within the next six months.

He felt sure she knew, or could meet if she so wished, plenty of charming, eligible men amongst whom she might find a suitable mate. He proposed to settle a generous income on the man on the day of his marriage to Billie.

If, on the other and, Billie defied him and persisted with her outrageous views upon matrimony, she must face single bliss with poverty. In other words, he would stop her allowance and disinherit her if she were not married by the end of the summer.

This alarming letter made Vera wildly excited.

'Billie!' she gasped. 'My dear! What will you do?'

Billie, sitting on the edge of the bed, smoking, was outwardly not at all excited. But the slim hand that held the cigarette shook slightly.

'Uncle Silas is mad,' she said. 'Quite mad.'

'But he means it, Bill. You'll have to get married now.'

'I shall do nothing of the kind.'

Vera's pretty face went peony-red. Her heart sank. She foresaw disaster for herself ... Billie's money and independence gone ... she, Vera, having to work instead of enjoying this idle life of luxury.

'*Billie!*' she screamed. 'You *must!* You can't let Uncle Silas disinherit you.'

Billie pitched away her cigarette.

'You're wrong, Vera, if you think I'm going to bury all my prejudices against marriage just for the sake of the money,' she said, her grey-green eyes blazing. 'It's outrageous.'

'Billie, don't be a fool!' wailed Vera. 'You can't give up two thousand a year ... your horse ... your cars ... your bungalow ... the winters in Algiers ... the servants—everything ...'

Billie bit her lips.

'It sounds pretty awful,' she muttered.

'You'd have to work for your living. You'd hate it!' exclaimed Vera. 'Billie, surely you might find a man you could love and——'

'Never!' broke in Billie. 'I don't believe in love.'

'Well—a man you could be happy with.'

'No; I'm far too independent by nature. I couldn't bear the ties of marriage.'

'But you know Uncle Silas means what he says. A Carden never goes back on his word.'

'I know that,' said Billie grimly. 'So, at the end of six months, I shall be looking for a job.'

Vera clutched the girl's arm.

'Bill—don't be a little idiot. You *can't* forfeit all the Carden millions—just for the sake of a prejudice. You must find the right man between now and the autumn. You *must*.'

Billie stood up—very straight and slim, and certainly much paler than usual. 'No,' she said. 'I won't get married. I *won't*.'

It was a terrible evening. Vera talked, argued, pleaded, bullied in turns, until Billie's head ached. Finally Billie retired to bed feeling more unhappy than she had ever felt before in a hitherto careless, joyous life.

The words 'Marriage' and 'Husband' danced before her

17

vision in letters of fire—like demons, mocking at her.

'I won't marry—I won't,' she told herself again and again. And then she fell to thinking of her beloved car, her hunter, her dogs, her glorious independence; the old freedom to roam the world, knowing that she was to inherit Silas G. Carden's millions.

Tears—not of sentiment, but of sheer anger—rose to her eyes.

'I don't want to give up everything,' she sobbed. 'Uncle Silas is a brute. Oh, what am I going to do?'

Curiously enough, before she drifted into uneasy slumber, she remembered Richard Bromley.

'Some women are driven to marriage,' he had said . . . 'for the sake of a home and money . . .'

Here she was—Billie Carden—actually being driven to marriage! It was intolerable: she who had proclaimed to Richard Bromley that most marriages are mistakes and ought to end in divorce.

He had agreed with her; he had deemed her wise for cutting sentiment out of her life. What would he say to this? She had her choice between marriage and riches, and single bliss and poverty! Nine people out of ten would probably choose the former. Vera, for instance. Vera was *vox populi*. Vera, in her shoes, would commence the search for a husband to-morrow.

Billie buried a tear-stained, furious little face on her pillow.

'I won't—I won't—I won't,' she muttered. And then fell asleep and forgot all about it.

CHAPTER 4

SHE woke at six o'clock, and began to worry and puzzle over Silas G. Carden's letter again. She rose at seven and dressed. From her window she could see miles of Sussex Downs—golden, brown, purple in the early morning sunlight. It was a fresh, heavenly morning of May.

'I must get out in the fresh air—and think,' said Billie. 'I feel stifled.'

Vera was still sleeping in the adjoining bedroom. Noiselessly, Billie let herself out of the bungalow and slipped round to the garage. Her other car was there—her little scarlet racer.

'A jolly good run at sixty miles an hour will make me feel better,' Billie decided.

But as she cranked the car and listened to the deep throb and hum of the powerful engine, she felt sick at heart. She loved the little racer. That would have to go—with the blue and silver Vauxhall—with everything else—when the summer ended.

'Damn!' said Billie loudly.

She climbed into the car and steered it out of the garage on to the sunlit road, which was free from traffic so early in the day, and invited a little 'scorching.'

Having cleared twenty miles—and reached Arundel—her thoughts winged to Richard Bromley, and the cottage between Storrington and Parham. She was a creature of moods; as unconventional in her habits as in her opinions. She was seized with the sudden whim to give Richard Bromley an early-morning call, and tell him about the letter from Uncle Silas.

'It will be interesting to hear what he has to say,' she thought grimly. 'He's an anti-sentimentalist—like myself. Yes, I'll give him a call.'

When she neared Bromley's cottage, she was surprised to find another car outside the gate. Just as she was climbing out of the scarlet racer, the cottage door opened and two men walked down the flagged path—Richard and an older man, wearing prince-nez, who carried a small black bag.

'A doctor,' surmised Billie. 'Tony must be ill.'

Richard saw her; stared at her in amazement. He looked pale and haggard, as though he had been up all night.

'Miss Carden!' he exclaimed.

'Am I in the way?' she asked bluntly.

'Not at all. If you will just wait one moment——'

He broke off, bade good-bye to the doctor, who entered his car and drove off, then turned back to the girl again.

'This is very unexpected,' he said.

'I didn't mean to come,' she said. 'But I found myself at Arundel, so came on here. I—rather wanted to talk to you.'

'You won't find my company very inspiring,' he said, with a twisted smile. 'I'm feeling just like—hell!'

'That was a doctor,' she said. 'Is it—Tony?'

'Yes,' he said, pulling out is pipe and clenching his teeth on the stem. 'He was taken bad soon after I got back from Storrington yesterday, and I've been up with him all night. He's—very ill.'

'I'm terribly sorry,' said the girl.

'It's the devil,' said Richard, in a hoarse voice. 'You see—he needs an operation—a man from Harley Street—an expensive nursing-home. He'll probably die if he doesn't get them. He could go to a free hospital, but that would kill him. I know Tony. The very idea of a hospital and a public ward has always been a nightmare to him, and he made me swear I'd never send him to one. So what am I to do? Just sit here—and see him die!'

He drew a hand across his brow. Then he pulled himself

together and looked at the girl with his weary, bitter eyes. She wore the same boyish suit and shirt-blouse he had seen her in yesterday. He wondered vaguely what had brought her here this morning.

'There's nothing to be done for Tony at the moment,' he said. 'You—wanted to talk to me, you said. Can I be of any help to you?'

'I wouldn't have come had I known you were so worried,' she said. 'My trouble, compared to yours, is small.'

'Won't you come in?' he said. 'Perhaps I can offer you some breakfast.'

'No, thanks,' she said, with a slight laugh. 'I'm not hungry. But I'll come in for a moment and talk to you while you eat yours.'

Later, sitting by the open casement, with her face turned from the man who was attempting to make a meal, and was obviously too worried to do so, Billie confided her trouble in him.

'So you see,' she finished, 'I'm not quite the fortunate and independent young woman I appeared to be yesterday.'

Richard poured himself out some coffee. His brows were contracted.

'H'm,' he said. 'It's all very difficult. It seems to me a bit hard of Uncle Silas.'

'Rotten' said Billie hotly.

'And you've either got to take a husband within six months or—become one of this world's unhappy workers, eh?'

'So it appears.'

'H'm,' said Richard again. 'It's a bit of a snag—for a girl with your views.'

'You sympathised with my views yesterday. Now what do you say?'

'I still say marriage is all wrong, and that freedom is the best,' he observed. 'But if I were in your shoes——'

'Well?' she asked eagerly, her bright grey-green eyes turning to him.

'I'd find a husband, and stick to my thousands,' he said

grimly. 'To be poor is the very devil ... as I'm finding. And—it's worse for a girl than a man.'

'You'd marry—against all your prejudices—and after your experience?' she said incredulously.

'Yes——' He shrugged his shoulders. 'I would, if I were placed as you are, and could find a decent chap to strike a bargain with me ... for instance. I'd stipulate that I must be just as free after marriage as before.'

'No man would ever keep to that bargain,' said Billie scornfully.

'It depends on the man.'

She leaned her chin on her hand, and stared at him in silence a moment. Her heart was beating rather quickly.

'*It depends on the man* ...' That sentence reiterated in her mind. Yes, it was true. And if she could find a trustworthy man—a man who felt like she did about things and would agree to a union, in a cold-blooded, unsentimental way, just for the sake of the money ... then she would not have to give up her cars and her bungalow and her winters abroad—and poor little Vera would not be turned out to work, either ...

For a long, long space she sat there, silently ruminating, her eyes still fixed on Richard Bromley's tired, cynical face. Then suddenly a thought flashed through her brain ... her heart missed a beat ... raced on at absurd speed. She sucked in her breath.

Richard looked up at her.

'What are you going to do?' he asked. 'I'm interested.'

'Are you?' she said in a queer voice. '*How* interested?'

'What do you mean?' the tone of her voice and the expression in her eyes disconcerted him.

'I mean—doesn't the financial side of this question interest you—as much as the sentimental side?'

His own heart began to leap uncomfortably.

'My dear Miss Carden ...'

'Look here, Richard Bromley,' she broke in, with her boyish love of directness and simplicity, 'you've advised me to find a husband who would strike a sensible bargain with me and keep to it—and so retain my money. Now you dislike romance and have no belief in love—having suffered through a bad mistake. Also—you need money—for the boy upstairs. What would you say if I asked *you* to strike that bargain with me, and satisfy Uncle Silas?'

Richard stared at her in a stupefied way. Then, with flushing cheeks, he laughed and said:

'My God—are you suggesting that I—should—marry you?'

'Yes,' said Billie calmly. 'We both hate love and want the money. Wouldn't we make a perfect pair! Outwardly we would be husband and wife. In reality we would be free and independent of each other. It would be doing each other a good turn. What do you say?'

Richard rose to his feet and drew his beloved pipe out of his coat-pocket.

'My dear Miss Carden—I can only say that I think you are mad,' he said.

'Why mad?' said Billie quite calmly. 'Didn't you yourself advise me to find a man to strike that bargain with me?'

'I was not intimating that I wished to be the man.'

'You are insulted by the suggestion? Oh, come——!' Billie laughed and bit her lower lip. Her face was a trifle flushed now. 'Look here—let's talk about it without prejudice. I know I'm doing what very few women would do—in making such a proposition (it is proposition more than a proposal, you know!), but I've no false modesty or anything stupid like that. I want to keep my money. You yourself have said it's damnable to be poor. That boy upstairs wants money, and plenty of it, to cure him. We needn't worry each other or even occupy the same house, if we don't want to. It'll be a purely business arrangement. Will you think it over?'

CHAPTER 5

RICHARD'S first inclination was to put a speedy end to the conversation, and pooh-pooh the whole idea as absurd. In fact, he felt rather annoyed that this young woman should suggest that he should marry her for the sake of her money.

Then a sense of humour restored his balance. He felt rather amused and not at all angry. In the old days, before his manifold misfortunes had embittered him and turned him into a surly, gloomy individual, he had possessed a very strong sense of humour, and it was still there. Now, even in this hour of anxiety about his young brother, it returned. He sat down in his chair again and laughed outright.

'How damned funny!' he exclaimed.

It was Billie's turn to be angry.

'It's not in the least funny,' she said. 'It's quite serious.'

'That we should get married after a twenty-four hours' acquaintance, eh?'

'Well? If the arrangement is a business one without any sentiment attached to it, what does it matter whether you know a lot about me, or I about you? I shan't be required to put up with your bad temper at breakfast-time (if you've got one), and you won't be asked to admire me every time I put on a new hat.'

Richard thrust out his long legs, and laughed again.

''Pon my soul, you're the weirdest girl I've ever met.'

Billie moved her head impatiently.

'Don't waste time telling me I'm weird. Talk this out seriously,' she said. 'Talk about it just as though I were a man, proposing to take you into partnership—not a woman wanting to marry you. I don't want to marry you in the least. You know quite well the very idea of marriage horrifies me. But I've got to do it, or be disinherited by Uncle Silas; and I don't want to be poor. On your side, there's Tony. Wouldn't you like to see him in a first-class nursing-home in Wimpole Street, and all the rest of it?'

'Oh yes. But I can't quite relish the idea of the bills being paid by you,' Richard said dryly.

'By you,' contradicted Billie equally dryly. 'Uncle Silas proposes to settle an income on my—er—husband . . . on the day I marry him.'

'It sounds a bit better, but it's the same thing in the end, my dear child.'

'I'm not your dear child—I hate being patronised!' said Billie, springing to her feet. 'I'm trying to discuss this business with you like one fellow to another. But if you want to be just scornful and facetious—I'm off!'

She stood facing him, her hands in her coat-pockets, her brown, cropped hair flung back, eyes bright and angry glaring at him. He regarded her critically, trying not to show that he was amused since it annoyed her. But really, he thought, it was all deuced funny. Girl! Truly, she was more boy than girl. Yet when he visualised her in softer, more feminine clothing, with a softer expression (Richard, like most men with a temperament had a vivid imagination), he could see her a very pretty woman indeed. Her features were a trifle sharp—the nose too thin and the chin too pointed—but the eyes were amazingly beautiful with those thick lashes; and the mouth fine, generous, strongly moulded. He had put women out of his life long ago . . . since Olive, his wife, had left him. The girl, Billie Carden, was an interruption, a disturbance in his bachelor existence. He mistrusted all women now, and had firmly made up his mind to do without them.

Yet Billie was different. There was no nonsence about her. She demanded neither love nor flattery nor sentiment in any shape or form. She merely wanted a husband in name—so that she might retain the Carden fortune.

'Like one fellow to another ...' she had said. Well, why not? Why not discuss the thing in that spirit?

'Good-bye,' said Billie, turning on her heel.

'No—wait,' said Richard. 'I've changed my mind. I'll talk it over. I'm curious just to hear exactly what you would suggest doing if I decided to—enter into this cold-blooded partnership.'

'Pray don't consider me,' said Billie coldly. 'Think only of your own side of it—your need of the money. I put the idea before you, first for my own sake, because I know you hate sentiment as much as I do, and won't be sloppy over the business; and, secondly, for the sake of that poor kid upstairs.'

'Quite so,' said Richard. 'I didn't for an instant imagine you were enamoured of my manly beauty.'

'Cut that out,' said Billy. 'Now, what about it?'

'What are your plans?'

'I've none made. This is all on the spur of the moment. When I first read my uncle's letter, I decided to give up the money. The thought of marriage—real marriage—is unbearable to me. But a friendly partnership—a financial transaction—well, why not? Uncle Silas will be pleased.'

'He won't mind who the husband is? I'm a penniless author—not a titled bloke, y'know.'

'That's all right. He won't mind. He'll think it real love.'

Her sarcasm made the man smile.

'Cold-blooded little devil, but I rather admire her,' he reflected. Aloud he said: 'Your uncle would come over from America to inspect your choice as soon as you cable news of your engagement?'

'Yes. Then he'll want to witness the marriage, which would take place without any fuss at a registry office; then settle the money on you; then return to America, most likely.'

'And the happy couple?'

'Separate without letting Uncle Silas know it,' said Billie bluntly. 'Its a bit of a dirty trick, but we might meet

26

occasionally—play a round of golf or do a show in town—just to keep up our acquaintanceship. But I'd just as soon go on living with my cousin, and you can take Tony abroad.'

For the first time real interest flickered in Richard's tired blue eyes.

'By jove! it'd be good to see the boy fit and well, and to be able to take him to the South of France this winter,' he said.

'Well, it can be done. And I've no compunction in making it all a cut-and-dried affair behind my uncle's back. He has no right to force me into matrimony against my will. Anyhow—that's my affair. And you needn't go off the deep end about marrying a woman for her money, etc. etc., since it's all premeditated on both our parts and for Tony's sake.'

Richard was conscious of growing excitement. The thing had seemed ridiculous at first, and yet ... Billie's cool, practical scheme was beginning to attract, to tempt him. Certainly it would not be 'doing her down,' he mused. It was her own idea. And it would not be like putting a woman in Olive's shoes, risking a second matrimonial disaster. By law, this girl, Billie, would be Mrs. Richard Bromley ...by mutual pact, they would be mere friends. Why not accept the offer—strike the bargain—for Tony?

'Look here,' he said, suddenly breaking the silence that had fallen between them, 'I'm looking at it from every point of view. I can see that Tony and I will benefit considerably if I—we marry. But I'm a man, and I take no risks. It's always the woman who takes the risk. You like to be thought of as a boy, but you're a girl. Aren't you making a rather reckless offer? Why should you trust me to keep to my share of the bargain, for instance? You've only known me a few hours. I might be a liar, a drunkard, a cad—any sort of a fellow.'

Billie mused upon this, then looked at him frankly, the suspicion of a smile curving her lips.

'Yes, you might be. But I pride myself on being rather a judge of character. I'm not easily taken in by people. I think you're straight. That's all that matters. So long as you keep your promise, I really don't mind whether you spend all the money on drink, dope, or racing. I'd prefer you not to do anything too outrageous and come into the public eye too much as I'd have to bear your name.'

Richard shook with silent mirth.

'I might promise not to do anything like that. I'm a moderate drinker, as a matter of fact. I wash out dope. I have a bet on a horse occasionally—or used to when I had money to waste. I used also to have the reputation for liking pretty women.'

'I should think you've had your lesson there,' said Billie dryly.

'I have,' he said. The laughter sped from his face, and left him haggard and cynical again. 'No—I dare say you won't take much risk. I shan't break my word to you if I give it. We would cut the word "love" right out of our marriage.'

'We would,' said Billie. Then she added in a more kindly tone than she had hitherto used, 'You understand me, Richard Bromley, and I think I understand you. We might be good friends, one day.'

He stood up, walked to the window, and stared out at the sunlit little garden. He was no longer thinking of Billie or of himself, but of the boy upstairs who lay on his bed racked with pain, and so terribly in need of the money which Silas G. Carden would settle upon his niece's husband on the day he married her. The temptation to accept it, to fall in with this girl's plans, was increasing with every passing moment.

The urge of present need for Tony was upon him. He was really indifferent as to the future. Billie Carden's offer had come at the psychological moment—when he was crazy with worry over the boy whom he loved better than anybody, anything on earth. A reckless vein ran through Richard Bromley. This strange, proposed marriage with a girl who intends to be just 'a friend' might turn out a success ... might end in disaster. Who could tell? Fate had juggled with him in the past. He was not particularly happy or contented. Why not juggle with Fate in his turn—and hope for the best?

28

He thrust a hand in his pocket—pulled out half a crown.

'Heads I do it—tails I don't,' he muttered.

He spun the coin, clapped it on the back of one hand, looked at it.

Billie, watching him with a curious feeling of excitement, although her sun-browned face was calm, as unconcerned as ever, said:

'Well—which is it?'

He turned round—with the look of a fatalist, showed her the coin.

'Heads!' she said, with indrawn breath.

'Yes. I do it. If you're absolutely certain of what you're in for—of what you're proposing to do—I'll enter into this financial transaction which we must call an engagement and wedding.'

'I know what I'm doing,' said Billie, her eyes very bright. She looked straight into the man's blue eyes. 'It's a bargain. No going back for either of us,' she added.

'Very well,' he said. 'Kismet! We are now, I take it, engaged!'

She gave a short, amused laugh.

'I suppose we are—yes.'

'Rapid business, what? Two meetings—and an engagement.'

'I will cable to Uncle Silas as soon as I get home,' she said. 'He will then sail for England at once to make sure I'm telling the truth, and we'll have to get married. Meanwhile, I don't want the boy to wait about. He must be driven up to town, and taken to a home at once.'

Richard's eyes softened.

'It's very decent of you to think of Tony,' he began. But Billie, very red in the cheeks, interrupted:

'Please don't thank me now or ever for anything that is done for Tony. It's all part of the business, and in exchange you are enabling me to keep my money. There it is—a question of mutual gratitude—so we can cut out the thanks on both sides.'

He was forced to admire her. She was as simple, as direct, as consistent in her methods as he could have expected any man to be over a business concern.

'Right you are,' he said, 'And look here—Tony isn't like we are. He's a dear, sentimental ass. If he thought we were marrying for these reasons, it'd worry him to death.'

'Don't tell him. Let him think what he wants. Tell him it's love at first sight! I don't mind. Now I'm going home. I'd like you to see your doctor and find out when Tony can be moved to town. My Vauxhall is beautifully sprung—we can take him up in that. Meanwhile, if you can come over to my bungalow on your motor-bike, after lunch, for an hour, I'd like you to meet my cousin, Miss Disney, who will be "in the know" about this.'

'Very well,' said Richard. 'My woman, Mrs. Judd, will stay in with the boy, and I needn't be gone long.'

'Good-bye, then, till this afternoon—Richard.' She used the Christian name bluntly—held out her hand.

He took it, conscious of a queer thrill from that tight, hard little grip of her fingers. How strong they were, in spite of their slenderness. It was a handshake on their compact. He knew it. The world seemed to have turned upside down for him. He ... of all men ... to be engaged ... to be arranging a marriage with this girl who was a comparative stranger! It was extraordinary.

'Good-bye—Billie,' he said.

CHAPTER 6

BILLIE went back to her bungalow in the scarlet racer at a dangerous and unlawful speed, feeling much as Richard felt. Her world was upside down. She burst in upon Vera, who was breakfasting in bed and reading a paper, and calmly announced her engagement to Mr. Richard Bromley, of Tudor Cottage, near Storrington.

'*Billie!*' shrieked Vera.

Billie flung off her hat and sat down on the edge of the bed, smoothing back her glossy brown hair. The expression on her face might almost have been called sheepish.

'Well, there you are, my dear ... your own advice. Marriage rather than give up the Carden millions.'

'But, *Billie* ...' Vera leaned forward and clutched her arm. 'You mean it? You're not joking? You're engaged ... to that man you met yesterday?'

'I am.'

Vera fell back on the pillow and simulated a swoon, then burst into hysterical laughter. Tears of combined mirth and astonishment filled her eyes. She ruffled her pretty golden hair until it stood out like an aureole framing a rose-flushed face.

Billy hunched her shoulders at this, seized upon a cigarette and lit it, smoked rather fiercely for a moment. Then she said:

'I seem to be an object of amusement to everybody to-day. However—laugh away! Facts remain. I'm engaged. And it's not so funny for me, my dear Vera. I shall writhe at the congratulations that will be pouring on me from all parts of the globe in a few weeks—to say nothing of my tiresome uncle's blessing, and the awful business of getting married!'

Vera sat up again. She was solemn now. Her eyes were wide with excitement. Billie, glancing at her thoughtfully, decided that Vera was really very pretty. A pity she was not going to be the bride. Vera could have done it all so well—blushes, heart-burns, flutters—the real thing!

'Lord, what a bride I shall be!' Billie contemplated. 'Entirely without emotion, and completely bored. I'd rather go to a tea-fight ... and that's bad enough!'

Vera was piling her with questions now.

'How did you bring it off? How *could* you have fixed it all up so quickly? When are you to be married? What does Mr. Bromley think of it? Is it a strictly business affair, or are you in love with each other ... ?'

'My dear Vera!' Billie stopped her, in a tone of disgust. 'Am I likely to be *in love*? What is love? You know my views on it. No—Richard Bromley and I are striking a cool bargain. Now keep quiet a minute, and don't wriggle about like that and get so flushed and excited. It's too early in the morning. I'll tell you everything if you'll listen without any of your fatuous interruptions.'

Vera subsided. Any rudeness from her cousin reduced her to a pricked bubble. She shrugged her white and shapely shoulders, lay back in the pillows again, and listened. So she heard exactly why and how Billie's engagement had come about.

'It's all very original and extraordinary,' was her observation when Billie ceased talking. 'What a strange man Richard Bromley must be.'

'Oh no—only a bit more sensible than most.'

'Because he holds your awful, unnatural views about cutting out love and sentiment?'

'Yes,' said Billie coolly.

'H'm,' said Vera. 'I still think he is strange. So are you. A good pair you'll be. But I've never yet met the man who could keep a promise like that. You try to ape the boy, my dear, but you're a jolly attractive girl in spite of it, and if when he's married you he doesn't want to make love to you——'

'Oh, you make me sick!' broke in Billie, springing to her feet and throwing her half-smoked cigarette out of the open casement window with an angry gesture. Her cheeks were scarlet. 'You can never look at or talk to a man without thinking in terms of sex.'

Vera bit her lip, but smiled to herself.

'I'm an ordinary woman.'

'And if you didn't live with some one like myself who can keep you in order, you'd be a beastly little flirt.'

Vera knew this to be perfectly true. She did not like the

truth. However, she kept her temper admirably with Billie. Billie was 'chancellor of the exchequer.' And really, whatever the mad girl chose to do, it was a relief to realise that she meant to retain her fortune and comply with Uncle Silas's request.

'Oh well, Bill,' she said, with a sweet smile, 'never mind about poor little me or whose views are correct. The fact remains that you are going to marry this man. I hope for your sake, darling, it will be a success. And if you trust him——'

'I do,' said Billie, narrowing her eyes and visualising the man she had just left. 'I think he is straight. Don't forget he had to divorce his wife, who ran away from him with a Guardee just when he was down and out and most needed her. That's enough to put him off love, surely!'

Vera raised delicately pencilled brows, but made no response. In her very feminine heart she believed implicitly in the power of sex ... the power of a pretty woman over a man. No matter if he possessed the strength of a St. Anthony; in the end, woman conquered. Richard Bromley was no exception. Anyhow, this affair had a spice of excitement in it for Vera. She wanted to meet the strong, silent, embittered Richard. It was going to be fun.

'He is coming here after lunch to meet you,' said Billie, 'so bring out your weapons—your war-paint and Paris get-up, etc., old thing! Only I don't advise you to set out too strongly to war against his frigid and cynical views upon love. You might win. Then he'd marry you instead of me, and the money would go West! Bye-bye ... I'm off to the golf-links.'

Vera stared after her cousin's retreating form.

'Little brute!' she muttered viciously. 'Always sneering at sentiment! One day she'll get punished. I hope she will. As for this Richard Bromley ... I expect he'll be hateful, and I shall be bored stiff!'

But when the said Richard Bromley arrived at The Hollow—Billie Carden's bungalow on the Downs—Vera changed her mind. It was some considerable time since she had met a man as attractive as Richard. He was a surly brute, certainly—but a remarkably good-looking one. How Billie could become engaged to him and not fall in love, Vera could not think.

Billie was in the garage, tinkering with her scarlet racer, so Vera received Richard in the pretty, cool, green and lavender drawing-room. She, exquisite in a flowered ninon dress, sleeveless, very chic, very French, held out her hand and smiled radiantly up at the black-haired, blue-eyed giant who was staring at her with a dubious expression.

'You are Mr. Bromley—Billie's fiancé?' she murmured. 'How simply marvellous. Do sit down. I'm Vera Disney. Billie and I have lived together for years, so we're sure to see a lot of each other in the future.'

'Oh—er—yes,' said Richard vaguely, and sat down.

Vera offered him a cigarette, then lit one herself, and smoked it in a long amber holder. Vera did everything gracefully. She always managed to fall into the best possible poses for effect. In this moment she reclined on a Chesterfield, her golden head against a large black silk cushion, quite conscious that the flowered gossamer frock was very short and showed a great deal of pretty, silken legs, and that the way in which she was smiling at Richard Bromley from beneath long lashes was particularly engaging.

Richard, however, gave one look at Vera Disney, then stared round the room. He was not at all in the mood to be thrilled by a very pretty young woman. He was too worried about Tony, and interested in his strange engagement to Billie Carden. Miss Disney, he gloomily mused, was the perfectly produced vampire of the modern age who sucked the time, the money, and the heart of foolish man. Olive, his faithless wife, had been fair, chic, charming ... rather like this girl. No; he had no use for her.

Politely he conversed with her, but with much more interest studied the room. The bungalow was Billie Carden's choice, and he was curious to see in what direction her taste lay. The green and lavender drawing-room was simple enough to please him. It was furnished in old cottage style—pale mauve casement curtains—a couple of good rugs on a polished oaken floor. There were one or two decent pieces of furniture, he reflected. He liked that well-polished antique dutch desk near the open red-tiled fireplace; the old oak chest which bore a huge copper jug full of blue-bells and pale green leaves through which the spring sunlight filtered goldenly. There were four pictures on the grey walls—all of which Richard (who prided himself upon being a judge of these things) pronounced 'very decent.' Two were etchings, two delicate water-colours.

A baby-grand Bluthner piano occupied one corner of the room, strewn with music. That was surely Miss Disney's toy, thought Richard. He could not imagine Billie at the piano. But the thing in the room which most interested him was a full-length photograph of a woman in evening-dress. It stood on the mantelpiece between two old beaten-brass candlesticks. The pose was a peculiarly graceful one, and the woman, wearing a long, flowing dress which sloped off the shoulders, was of the past generation. She was very beautiful—a noble head, waving hair looped at the nape of the neck—lovely, soft eyes.

Richard got up and stood before this photograph, fascinated by the queer resemblance between the woman—so gentle, so feminine—and Billie.

'Who is that, Miss Disney?' he asked.

And he was not surprised when Vera said:

'Oh, that's Billie's mother. She died years ago—soon after Billie was born. But Billie loves that photo—carries it about with her everywhere.'

'Ah,' thought Richard. 'So she has a soft spot in her somewhere. Well—she is sensible to reserve it for her mother.'

Richard idolised the memory of his own dead mother. He liked Billie for cherishing the memory of hers. In a dim, queer way he saw the girl in every line of the pictured face. Put her in that flowing gown, let her cropped brown hair grow long, let the firm young lips soften into the gracious smile on the lips of Billie's mother ...

Billie came into the drawing-room, and rudely dispelled Richard's illusion. Almost with a shock he surveyed her. She was in blue overalls, like any lad at a garage, hair awry, small hands covered in oil, cheeks smudged and flushed.

'Oh, hullo!' she said, wiping away a lock of brown hair and leaving a fresh smear of oil on her forehead. 'Sorry I'm in the middle of this job, but I must finish it before tea. I've got two plugs sooted right up. Is Vera looking after you?'

'I'm trying to. But do hurry up, darling,' cooed Vera from the sofa.

Richard uttered a short laugh and turned away from Mrs. Carden's photograph. Her daughter, in this moment anyhow, looked as though she could never be anything but a boy.

'I'm all right, thanks,' he said. 'Enjoying looking round. Can I help with the car?'

'No—I'll be finished in five minutes. How is Tony?'

'A bit better—not so much pain this afternoon,' said Richard. 'The doctor thinks he can be moved up to town at the end of the week without any harm.'

'Good,' said Billie. 'We'll drive him up on Saturday, then. If you agree, I'll go up to town to-morrow and talk to a man I know who is a first-rate surgeon, and has a home in Wimpole Street. Sir Basil Graham. Heard of him?'

'Oh yes, indeed. And you know him? You think he'd take Tony's case?' said Richard, with sudden light in his tired eyes.

'Sure to. anyhow, I'll run up and see.'

'Thanks very much,' said Richard.

CHAPTER 7

THE quaint, slim little figure in the stained blue overalls disappeared. Richard was left to the mercy of the beautiful Vera, with whom he was not nearly so much at ease. He could deal with Billie just as he would deal with a lad. But he was sagacious enough to realise that, with girls of Vera's type, a man can never deal—in safety.

He was embarrassed by her prettiness, by her charm, by her flow of light conversation. It savoured too much of Olive. What an idiot he had made of himself over Olive ... till the very hour she had left him. God! he didn't want to be reminded of her. It hurt too badly, even now. He was relieved when Billie returned; Billie who had discarded the overalls and scrubbed her face and hands, and appeared at tea in one of her usual boyish shirts with a green tie that made her eyes look quite green, and a short-well-tailored skirt.

Vera ate the sandwiches and cakes. Richard and Billie drank tea and smoked cigarettes. The topic of conversation was now entirely cars. Cars Billie had tried, had sold, had bought, had smashed ... heaven knew what Billie had not done with cars! Richard was amused. Vera was bored. Finally, Vera left the other two and retired to her bedroom to fetch a hat and drive herself into Brighton. They were the most ridiculous engaged couple she had ever seen. The whole thing was preposterous!

Left alone with Billy, Richard suddenly drew a small box from his coat-pocket and thrust it into her hand.

'What on earth's this?' she exclaimed.

Rather red in the face, he explained:

'I looked it up after you'd gone. I thought, as your uncle is coming over, he'd expect to find you with a—a—er—engagement ring. This ring was my mother's—not my wife's. Wear it—if you like.'

Billie was astonished and altogether embarrassed. She looked at the ring—a single pearl of no great value—but charmingly set. In it was an inscription—*Laura Mary Bromley*, 1888.

'Don't wear it if you'd rather not,' said Richard hastily.

'Oh, why not?' said Billie, with equal haste. 'I—I don't mind. Of course I'll wear it. Thanks very much.'

He watched her slip it on her slender brown finger, and smiled a trifle dryly. The little old-fashioned pearl looked oddly white and feminine against her skin, which was so boyishly tanned. He had offered that ring to Olive in the early days of his disastrous marriage, and she had refused it. It had been too simple, too innocent for her taste. She had always worn bizarre jewellery—great gleaming rings of French paste, antique, conspicuous. She had possessed a lovely white dimpled hand to show them off.

Richard thrust the thought of Olive away from him. Why, he reflected savagely, must he always remember things about the woman who had run away from him? He centred his attention upon Billie again—Billie whom he was going to marry for cold, hard, practical reasons. She was still evidently embarrassed by the ring which was to be the outward sign of their engagement, and was twisting it round and round her finger. Then she pulled a packet of cigarettes from the pocket of her skirt and lit one.

'It's a pretty ring,' she said. 'Fits me, doesn't it?'

'Oh, quite well,' he said.

'I don't suppose I shall wear it often,' she said cheerfully. 'It would be a pity to hurt the pearl, as I tinker about with my bus in the garage, and that sort of thing.'

'I don't mind in the least when you wear it,' said Richard,

shrugging his shoulders. 'It's more for Uncle Silas than anybody.'

'Poor Uncle Silas!' said Billie, her eyes twinkling. 'What a rotten pair of tricksters we are, really—deceiving the poor old man into believing us a fond young couple.'

'We haven't deceived him yet,' said Richard, a trifle gloomily. 'And he might make things more difficult for us than we imagine, once he arrives.'

'We'll risk that,' said Billie., 'Besides, we've agreed that ours is a purely mercenary transaction, and we can't allow sentimental pity for Uncle Silas to upset us.'

Richard sat back in his chair and grinned, and she suddenly grinned at him in response. A little warm wave of good humour and friendliness passed between them. Then suddenly Billie said:

'I hope my cousin Vera entertained you nicely while I was in the garage?'

'Oh, certainly.'

'She's very pretty and attractive, isn't she?'

'I suppose so,' said Richard. 'But to be frank, she isn't the type I admire.'

'And what type do you admire?' inquired Billie.

He hesitated. Then his cynical eyes sped to the photograph of Mrs. Carden between the brass candlesticks.

'I admire that type immensely,' he said, nodding toward it. 'But it's of a generation that's passed, and hard to find amongst the shingled, masculine young women of to-day.'

Billie sat still for a moment, staring hard at her mother's photograph, her cigarette burning away to ash, forgotten. Hard to find ... yes, practically impossible to find a woman like the young mother who had died when she, Billie, was a little child. Mrs. Carden had been swept away suddenly, tragically, by pneumonia one severe winter out in Ohio, when Billie was three years old. Yet she dimly recollected sweet moments when she had been gathered to that beautiful young mother's heart ... dimly remembered the soft lovely eyes shining down at her, the noble head with its wealth of brown hair, coiled at the nape of the neck ... just as that photograph depicted. Through all the years that had passed, Billie had wanted her mother, missed the tender maternal care she had never received from the expensive governess her father had engaged for her, or at the smart college to which she had later been sent to complete her education.

It was the one sentimental spot in Billie's heart—her love and memory of her mother. When she turned to look at the man again, her face bore the expression of one who had been treading sacred aisles.

'I quite agree with you,' she said. 'My mother was exquisite, and I am not at all surprised you should admire her type. I should say it is not only hard to find, but extinct.'

He frowned slightly. It was on the tip of his tongue to tell her that he had only just been thinking that she would resemble her mother accurately were she to let her hair grow and wear a flowing old-fashioned gown. But he desisted. The look in Billie's eyes embarrassed him. Better to keep off the conversation of the mother she so obvious adored. She was the first to change. With a quick movement she flung her cigarette into the grate, and sprang to her feet.

'Don't let's sit indoors while the sun is shining. Come and see what there is of the garden,' she said abruptly.

He followed her out of the bungalow.

Before Richard went home, the conversation was turned to the subject of Tony.

'I'll drive up to town to-morrow morning and see Sir Basil Graham,' Billie said. She had walked to the gate of The Hollow to see Richard off. He was preparing to mount his dilapidated motor-bike. 'Then I'll drop in to see you later in the day, and tell you the plans.'

'I shall be most grateful,' he said.

She let her gaze rest on him a moment, and thought how tired and haggard his face appeared in the vivid sunlight.

'Don't worry too much over the boy,' she said. 'Graham will give him a new lease of life, I feel confident.'

'I hope you're right,' said Richard. 'The poor kid's had a rotten time lately.'

He looked up from the bike to the girl, then dropped his gaze again swiftly, flushing red.

'I can't quite get used to the idea of you doing all this, letting you pay, when I haven't a bean——' he began to mutter.

'Now, my dear Richard, stop that!' interrupted Billie curtly. 'A bargain's a bargain, and I shouldn't be keeping a bean of my fortune if you hadn't agreed to marry me. Here am I most effectively engaged, with ring and all . . .' she held up her hand and exhibited the little pearl, laughing. 'Don't let either of us become pained or distressed. So long.'

He laughed with her. She had the knack of restoring him at once to good humour and confidence. He could not feel a swine about money when she put things like that. She was a good sport. He felt intensely grateful to her, because of Tony. And he was still more grateful when, twenty-four hours later, she drove down from London to his cottage and told him that she had interviewed the great surgeon and arranged for Tony's operation.

'I've engaged a room for him in Graham's nursing-home, and we are to drive the boy up on Saturday,' she said. 'I thought you'd like to be near him till the operation's safely over, so I booked a room for you at Ford's hotel. They know me there. Is that all right, friend Richard?'

Richard gasped a little.

'You're an extraordinary young woman,' he declared. 'You do take a fellow's breath away at the rate and determination with which you do things.'

'Oh, I can't stand fussing and hesitating,' said she. 'I agree that "He who hesitates is lost."'

'Well I'm in your hands over this,' he said dryly. 'It's all very generous of you, but I don't see how I can afford to stay at Ford's Hotel, nor can I allow you to pay the bill.'

Billie, pacing with her usual restiveness up and down Richard's sitting-room, paused before him and glared at him.

'I shall be furious if you continue to argue or discuss this money question,' she said. 'For once and for all, Richard, it's a bargain ... the share I'm carrying out. You'll have to do your share, once Uncle Silas arrives—never fear! I shall not pay your bill for you. You shall pay your own. I don't doubt you possess a bank, even if your balance is nil. I shall send you a cheque for one hundred to see you through Tony's illness. I mean for your expenses, not his.'

Richard dropped limply into a chair.

'The way you wealthy young women write off cheques for cool hundreds!' he exclaimed, rolling his eyes heavenwards.

'Better to spend my hundreds by doing something worth doing than just wasting it on pleasure-seeking,' she said bluntly. 'Well, that's that. Agreed?'

'I suppose so,' he said helplessly.

'I've had a cable from New York,' she added. 'My Uncle arrives in England in a fortnight's time.'

'Then I really shall begin to feel nervous,' said Richard.

'Don't worry—there'll be no walking up the aisle for me in orange-blossoms and veil, to meet you in frock-coat and silk hat. We'll have a cut-and-dried affair in a registry office.'

'Splendid,' said Richard.

He stared at Billie as he might have done at some extraordinary phenomenon. She was walking up and down the pretty sunlit sitting-room again, smoking the inevitable cigarette. She was rather a chic Billie to-day—perhaps had taken a little extra care of her appearance because she had been up to town. But her clothes were still severe, and without frills or fancies. She wore a perfectly tailored black coat and skirt, a white silk jumper with an Eton collar and red tie. The cropped brown head was hidden under a close-fitting hat of black felt, with a diamond arrow through the brim. Silk stockings and narrow American shoes completed a very smart toilette. Richard tried hard to realise that he was engaged to be married to this expensive-looking young woman. He felt almost horrified when he considered his shabby suit, his scanty wardrobe upstairs. He felt totally unfit to be the fiancé of Miss Billie Carden.

'Oh, lord, what have I taken on?' he reflected. 'If it weren't for Tony, I'd bunk out of this. It frightens me.'

42

It could not truly be said, however, that Richard looked or felt frightened when, a few minutes later, he drank a whisky-and-soda, and watched Billie drink one. It was half-past six and she was hot and thirsty after the long drive from town. She was as easy to 'drink with' and talk to as any boy. They made the final arrangements for taking Tony up to town. Billie would come in the Vauxhall for him immediately after breakfast on Saturday.

Before she departed she went upstairs to see Tony. He was not very well, but his thin, girlish face flushed with excitement when she entered the bedroom.

'Don't dare to try and sit up,' she said gaily, taking a chair beside him. 'And how's Tony to-day?'

'Oh, the pain's been beastly,' he said. 'But it's easier to-night. I say, is it true you're going to marry my brother?'

'Quite true,' said Billie. She held up her left hand. 'Doesn't that convey anything to you, Tony?'

The boy's violet-blue eyes opened wide.

'Gosh! It's our mother's ring,' he said in a hushed voice.

'Yes. Richard gave it to me yesterday.'

'Then you really are going to marry him! I say, it's a frightful surprise. I thought Dick hated women and never meant to marry again.'

'Ah, but my charm and beauty have wooed him from his resolve,' said Billie, in a dramatic tone.

Tony stared hard at her.

'But you hardly know each other, and I felt sure Dick wouldn't marry again after—after what happened. You know that rotten wife of his (I always hated her) let him down abominably and——'

'I know,' said Billie, growing serious. 'But my dear, don't get excited—it isn't good for you. Just lie quiet and listen to me. You needn't worry about your Dick. He'll be all right this time. He won't be let down, anyhow.'

'No, I don't believe you would let him down,' said the boy. 'I rather like you, Billie. You're not Olive's sort. You're a sport.'

She felt strangely moved, and wanted to lean down and

kiss the flushed, delicate face of the crippled boy. He looked so young, so pathetic with his curly head, his long-lashed eyes. He surely needed a woman's tenderness and care. But she found it impossible to respond to the maternal urge in her. From lifelong habit, she was boyishly opposed to exhibiting emotion. She thrust out a hand and took his.

'Thanks, old chap,' she said. 'I know we're going to be pals, anyhow.'

'Richard told me last night all that you were doing, or rather going to do, for me,' said Tony. 'You can't think what it means to me. If the op's a success and I can walk about again——' He broke off, husky with emotion.

'I quite understand. It will be marvellous,' said Billie, squeezing his hand, then dropping it. 'And Sir Basil is a trump—he'll be awfully decent to you.'

'I'll tell you something,' said Tony. 'I've been laid up with this rotten spinal trouble so long, and been a drag on Dick and let him sweat away to keep me, that if only I could get fit and start to work and pay him back, I—oh, I'd be grateful to you all my life for giving me this chance.'

'That's all right,' said Billie, clearing her throat. 'I don't want you to be grateful. We'll be sort of related, won't we, Tony—when I'm married to your Richard?'

'Well, it's been a mighty swift engagement,' said Tony, smiling at her shyly. 'Love at first sight, eh?'

Billie mumbled something quite inaudible and felt her cheeks grow hot. At that moment Richard entered the bedroom. Tony greeted him excitedly:

'I can hardly believe you two are engaged. It's a huge surprise, Dick. By jove, after all the cynical things you've said about women, too!'

'M'm,' said Richard, avoiding Billie's gaze.

'Still, Billie's different from most women I've met,' added Tony.

'Quite,' said Richard.

Billie hurriedly rose.

'I must get back to The Hollow,' she said. 'Vera will be

sitting on the doorstep wondering where I am. I said I'd get back for tea, and here it is getting on for seven o'clock!'

'Come and see me soon again,' said Tony.

'To-morrow, if you like,' she said. 'And the next day I'm motoring you up to Wimpole Street,'

'I shall be darn glad to get rid of the pain,' he said, with a wry smile.

Downstairs, Billie said to Richard:

'The boy thinks we fell in love at first sight. Well, you wanted him to think it, didn't you?'

'Yes,' said Richard awkwardly. 'He'd be pretty fed up with me if he knew the truth, I dare say, and I don't want him to worry—I only want him to get well.'

'So do I,' she said. 'He's rather a dear.'

CHAPTER 8

RICHARD watched her drive away in the scarlet and silver racer, then returned to his young brother's bedside. Tony was eating a scrambled egg—the early supper prepared for him by Mrs. Judd. Over this meal he waxed sentimental about his new sister-in-law to be.

'She's a wonderful girl—such a ripping good sort, Dick. Tell me more about your engagement. When did you first fall in love? And how did you dare tell her you loved her when she's got so much cash and we're so poor?'

Richard felt slightly flummoxed by this question. He fumbled for his pipe and stuck it in the corner of his mouth.

'Oh—I—er—I'm sure I don't know, Tony.'

'Well, it doesn't matter,' said Tony. 'I know you'd never marry a woman for her money. You aren't like that.'

The light in the little cottage bedroom was failing. The

purple mists of summer twilight were creeping over the garden, and in the kindly dusk the flush that mounted to Richard's cheeks was unnoticed by his brother. And if Richard was dumb on the subject of Billie, Tony told himself that it was because he was so deeply in love he found it hard to discuss her. Very right, very natural. And if Billie had money, she was at least doing the very best thing for herself, in Tony's eyes, by marrying Richard. His brother was the most wonderful person in the world to Tony.

The conversation which took place that same evening between Billie and her cousin Vera was very different. There was no necessity for lies where Vera was concerned. She knew the unvarnished truth about the surprising engagement between Billie and the perfectly strange young man she had encountered in a storm on the Storrington Road.

'I've never seen anything so ridiculous as you and your Richard,' Vera remarked, with a sniff, as she sat in the drawing -room drinking after-dinner coffee with her cousin.

'Why ridiculous?' inquired Billie.

'Well, you're so chilly and distant with each other.'

'Not at all. We're the best of friends. We aren't a loving couple, such as you would like us to be, dear Vera, but then, as you know, I don't believe in love, and am not marrying Richard Bromley for love.'

Vera drew a Spanish embroidered shawl closer about pretty bare shoulders, and shuddered.

'Your cold-blooded methods appal me,' she said.

Billie gave a dry laugh.

'I'm quite sure if it were your engagement you'd be holding his hand and kissing him round the corner,' she said.

'Well, so I would,' said Vera defiantly. 'I think he's almost as cold-blooded as yourself, now, but he wouldn't be if he were wakened up. He's awfully handsome.'

'Well, I prefer him unawakened,' said Billie dryly. 'However, I'm glad you approve of my choice.'

'Do you intend to remain like this after you've married him?' asked Vera curiously.

'Indeed, I do.'

'Heavens, how dull!'

'I leave the "roses and raptures" and thrills of life in *that* respect to you, my child,' said Billie.

Vera twisted her mouth.

'I suppose I shall be chucked out when you're Mrs. Bromley,' she said tentatively.

'I really don't know what will happen,' was the reply. 'But I don't suppose for a moment you will be "chucked out", stupid.'

'Thank goodness for that,' thought Vera.

She contemplated the possibility of making her home with Billie and Richard ... with some excitement. He was very good-looking with his blue eyes and black hair. He might get tired of cold, hard friendship ... might be willing to snatch a thrill from life with *her*.

'Who knows?' she said aloud.

'Who knows what?' said Billie lifting her head from the pages of the *Autocar*.

'Nothing,' said Vera, in her silkiest voice; and advancing to the piano, she sat down and began to play 'Tea for Two' very softly, singing the words under her breath.

Vera did not find herself very much the centre of things during the next few days, however. She was left to entertain herself as best she could at The Hollow while her cousin conducted Tony Bromley to town.

During that drive from Storrington to London in the big, beautifully sprung Vauxhall, Richard came to the conclusion that Billie was a fine and trustworthy driver. They arrived at Wimpole Street without a hitch, and Tony, lying on cushions at the back, with soft rugs around him, praised Billie with enthusiasm. Only twice did slight jolting intensify the pain in his back.

Directly he arrived at the big expensive nursing-home which belonged to Sir Basil Graham, he was given over to the care of a special nurse and put to bed in a spacious bedroom which awaited him, full of roses and carnations.

'Miss Carden sent them in,' the nurse announced.

Tony felt a lump in his throat, and looked at his brother who had come up with him, leaving Billie down in the waiting-room.

'How topping of her,' he said huskily.

'Yes,' said Richard, more moved than he cared to admit by this kindness to his young brother.

He left Tony with the nurse, quite happy and comfortable in his new bed, a pile of the latest magazines beside him, and great bowls and vases full of fragrant flowers to delight his eyes—all gifts from Billie Carden.

Then Richard, in another room, was introduced to the great surgeon himself, who had dropped in for a moment to see his new patient. He was a small, spare man with grey hair and keen dark eyes. He gave Richard at once the feeling of confidence that he so sorely needed. The thought of Tony's serious operation was weighing rather heavily upon him. Since the departure of Olive, Richard had given all his affection to the brother who had always seemed such a child. He had become father as well as brother to Tony after the death of their parents at the end of the War.

'You can be positive that I shall do my level best for the boy,' said Sir Basil. 'I can only judge from the report of your local doctor that an immediate operation is necessary. But I am going to make my examination this afternoon as soon as Tony has recovered from the fatigue of the journey, then I will telephone through to your hotel. Don't worry.'

'I won't,' said Richard.

'Talking of other things,' said the surgeon, 'I must congratulate you on your engagement to Miss Carden.'

'Oh—er—many thanks,' stammered Richard, clutching at his cigarette-case.

'I've known her some years. She's a very fine girl,' said Sir Basil. 'I was at school with her father. He was one of the best. I don't know the American uncle, but he seems a good fellow, and she's a lucky girl being his heiress. A dear child, too—so unspoiled by her good fortune.'

'Yes, quite,' said Richard.

Sir Basil surveyed him critically.

'Nice big healthy chap—good-looking, too,' he thought. 'The child hasn't chosen unwisely. He's well bred and seems intelligent, and that's more than I can say for most of the modern young men.'

Richard drove away from the nursing-home with Billie, in the Vauxhall.

'I'll drop you at Ford's,' she said. 'By the way, I've decided to stay in town, too, till Tony's operation is over. You won't want to grouse round town alone and mope. We'll do a dinner and show to-night, if you like.'

Richard looked at the sharp boyish profile of the girl, who was skillfully steering her big car through the traffic toward the hotel. Then he suddenly broke out:

'Look here, Billie, it's all very well. A bargain's a bargain, I agree. But I didn't agree that you should not only pay for my brother's operation, but buy him pounds' worth of flowers and fruit and papers, pay my hotel bill, take me out to dine . . .' He broke off with a gesture of protest.

She glanced swiftly at him. Then she smiled. She liked that hard, resolute look on his face.

'I respect your feelings,' she said. 'But do remember that I have sent you a cheque merely in advance, shall we say, for the service you are rendering me in becoming my—er—husband. You can cash it at the bank to-day, and pay your own bill and the dinner and show to-night.'

'If I take you out to a show and dinner, the money will not come out of that two hundred.'

'Where will it come from, then?' she grinned.

'My own earnings,' he said grimly. 'I sold a story the other day, and I can afford to take my fiancée out at least one night.'

'Right-o,' she said, with a cool little laugh. 'I'll respect that wish, my dear Richard. You shall waste your own money to-night.'

'Don't think I'm not grateful for all you've done for Tony,' he added more gently. But she cut him short.

'Any of that sort of talk and we'll really quarrel,' she declared. 'Here we are at Ford's. I'll drop you here. I'm going on to my Club in Dover Street—I shall put up there. Phone me during the afternoon and tell me what Graham says about Tony, and what time you want to fetch me this evening. So long!'

He got out of the car, and she drove away, waving a slender ungloved hand. He entered the hotel carrying his shabby suit-case and feeling very much like a man in a dream. What troubled him most at that moment was the thought of his dinner-jacket. It was horribly shabby. And it would seem so strange getting into it—going out in town again. The very last time he had worn his evening-suit and dined out in London had been with Olive—two weeks before she had left him. Since then he had lived the simple life in the country with his brother, and had disliked the thought of life up in town ... the feverish quest for pleasure that had meant so much more to his wife than *he* had meant to her. Now he was up here again; Tony was at Wimpole Street ... his fiancée was at her Club in Dover Street ... and to-night he would be taking her to dinner and to a show. It seemed incredible, unreal to Richard.

It seemed equally unreal and incredible to Billie Carden whenever she reviewed the situation during the rest of that day. Yet the thought of her engagement to Richard Bromley by no means appalled or worried her as the idea of marriage had done in the first place, when Uncle Silas had sent his ultimatum. She congratulated herself upon having found and chosen just the right man. She liked Richard—his hard, cynical, unemotional outlook suited her, harmonised with her own. Instinctively she trusted him, was certain that he would keep to his part of the compact. He was not the sort of man to break his given word. And she really quite liked his companionship. After all, let women boast of their equality to the male sex, indeed of their superiority—and in some cases Billie preferred women as companions. But there was no getting away from the fact that a strong, sensible masculine being like Richard Bromley was pleasing to have at one's side.

Having lunched at the club with the daughter of a peer (a girl whom Billie knew well, and who wore an 'Eton crop' and eyeglass, and drank an amazing number of cocktails without turning a hair), Billie felt almost antagonistic to her own sex, and welcomed the prospect of Richard as a companion that evening.

The Eton-shingled damsel gazed with horror at Billie's engagement ring.

'You—Billie Carden—going to marry!' she exclaimed, letting the eyeglass fall from her eye. 'What a catastrophe! We all thought you sensible, like we are—preferred your freedom—avoided this love-stuff. It'll be the ruin of you, my dear!'

'I'm not marrying for love, neither do I believe in it,' said Billie blandly. 'I'm marrying for the sake of retaining my money, if you want the straight truth, my dear Jo; and my husband will be a friend and nothing but a friend.'

Lady Jo smoothed back a satin-black head and pursed a mouth of amazing scarlet.

'Don't be too trustful, my child,' she drawled. 'No man is capable of marrying an attractive girl like yourself and remaining her *friend*.'

'Well, my fiancé is,' said Billie.

The argument that ensued left her rather annoyed but none the less confident in Richard.

Later that day he telephoned to her about Tony. Sir Basil had made his examination. Tony's case was serious, but he was confident of success, and was going to operate at ten o'clock the next morning.

'Good,' said Billie. 'Now, don't panic, Richard. Keep smiling.'

'I never panic,' said Richard indignantly. 'And I hate being spoken to as though I were a nervous baby.'

Billie stifled a laugh. She liked his spirit. He announced

that he had taken seats for a new Noel Coward production, and would call for her at the club at seven o'clock. They were to dine at The Kingfisher—a new, chic little restaurant just opened in the vicinity of Dover Street.

'But, my dear Richard!' protested Billie. 'You mustn't do that—The Kingfisher is frightfully expensive—ruinous, and——'

'How dare you?' broke in Richard, really angry. 'Just because I'm a poverty-stricken author it doesn't say I can't stand a woman a decent dinner. Did you think I was going to take you to an A.B.C.?'

He jerked the receiver up before she could apologise. She left the telephone box with a gleam of amusement in her eyes. Bravo for Richard! That was the stuff she liked. A pity that the absurd Lady Jo couldn't meet and contend with him; she would soon see that he was not the sort of man to get sloppy and let a woman down.

CHAPTER 9

AT seven o'clock Billie was ready for Richard in the vestibule of the Club. She experienced something approaching a thrill of pleasure when she saw him march in, undeniably handsome in spite of the shabby dinner-jacket—a fine, loose-limbed young man with a smooth brown face, resolute jaw, firmly shut mouth. His eyes looked extraordinarily blue to-night, and he seemed just a shade sulky; still annoyed because she had questioned his right to take her to The Kingfisher, she supposed. She met him with an impish grin.

'Good evening, Richard.'

'Oh—hullo!' he said shortly, and paused, staring at her rather foolishly. He had not recognized her. It was such an altered Billie; not the masculine young woman of the severe suit, or overalled-lad of the garage, but a feminine Billie in a black lace evening-gown and flame-velvet cloak with a roll chinchilla collar.

The close-cropped brown head was smoothly brushed, glossy as a chestnut. The frock was simple and plainly cut, and fashionably short. But it was a distinctly beautiful young woman who stood grinning so mischievously up at Richard, and for a moment her appearance startled, almost baffled him.

'My dear Richard!' she protested. 'Don't glare at me like that. I'm sure I'm very sorry I tried to stop you spending all your hard-earned gold.'

Her cool, level voice restored Richard's equilibrium. He bowed a trifle stiffly and turned toward the door.

'Don't worry about that,' he said. 'Come along. It's only a few steps down the road from this place.'

He was angry with himself rather than with her. Billie as a very pretty woman in evening-dress had momentarily disturbed him, and he realised he had had no right to be disturbed. She was still the same Billie. But it was something of a shock for him to realise how feminine she could be and was, beneath all the boyishness. And he was going to marry her. She would be his wife—only in name. Well, he could carry out his share of the bargain. She did not ask to be taken care of. Yet he began to wonder if she was really capable of taking care of herself where other men were concerned. She was so deuced attractive in this sort of attire.

During dinner, half-nervously he noticed the white, smooth beauty of her bare arms and slim young throat—like peeled almonds in contrast to the sun-tanned face. He saw other men at neighbouring tables stare at her. She was quite unconscious of admiration; was as natural, as direct, as matter-of-fact in speech and manner as ever. It was Richard who continued to feel ill at ease.

The last time he had dined in town, things had been so different. Olive had been with him—pretty, kittenish, dimpled—and he had thought her all his own . . . had felt so proud of her, so content with life.

All that had passed. Now he was a bitter, suspicious person. He was a very lonely and unhappy one, too, but that he refused to admit. He only knew, to-night, that he wished this girl whom he was about to marry had been ugly and uninspiring.

He ordered an excellent dinner for her, but he remained rather gruff and silent. She thought he was worrying about Tony; did not realise that this meal with her in the pretty restaurant, her new femininity, the gay music of the first-rate orchestra hurt him—reopened the wound his young wife had made when she had deserted him for a richer man. He had vowed to have nothing more to do with women. He wondered if he had been a fool to agree to Billie Carden's plan. Then he remembered the boy in the luxurious nursing-home, eagerly awaiting his release from the pain and misery he had borne for so many years. He softened. It was all for Tony's sake. He must carry on and grind with a ruthless heel the memories of a sentimental past.

He paid the bill and left The Kingfisher, glad to get out of the hot atmosphere into the cool summer starlight. Billie folded her cloak about her, and begged him not to take a taxi to the theatre.

'I like walking,' she said.

He was thankful, and walked at her side in a better frame of mind.

At the end of the play, which was amusing and interesting, he was quite cheerful again, and had forgotten to review the past or delve into psychological problems of the future. Billie had been in good form the whole evening, and he was bound to admit she was a charming companion.

She, on her part, had liked being with Richard, and thanked him with enthusiasm when she said good-bye outside her Club.

'It was ripping of you to give me such a decent time,' she said, holding out her hand. 'Good-night, and good luck to-morrow. You'll let me know at once when the op's over, won't you?'

'I will indeed. Good-night, and thanks for comming out with me,' he said.

They shook hands like comrades. For the second time since he had known her, he drew confidence from that firm, boyish clasp of her fingers. She, looking up at him, scoffed at the memory of Lady Jo's cynical outlook upon her engagement.

'One of these days your steely young man will lose his head and kiss you—then the fat will be in the fire!' had been one of Jo's remarks.

Billie regarded her fiancé's face, strong, dogged, rather splendid in the starlight, and smiled to herself. Richard was not the sort to lose his head. For an instant she imagined such a situation—Richard seizing her in his arms; that stern, firm mouth closing upon her own ...

A thrill of acute terror and dismay darted through her heart. She hastily muttered another good-night, and fled into the Club. Her cheeks were flame-colour, like her cloak.

'Heavens! I should hate him like poison if he ever did such an outrageous thing,' she told herself furiously.

It is a sad fact, however, that whatever one's thoughts or feelings may be during the day, one's dreams cannot be controlled. And that very night Billie dreamed that Richard Bromley was no longer a friend, a partner in a mercenary scheme, but a passionate lover. Those blue eyes of his were probing the very depths of her soul—she was held against his heart ...close, close ... and the kiss he laid on her lips neither terrified nor disgusted her. Neither did she hate him.

She awoke in the morning thoroughly indignant that such stupid dreams should be allowed to trouble a sensible young woman like herself.

'The sort of idiotic thing I should expect Vera to dream,' she reflected. 'Thank goodness it is never likely to come true!'

And just because of that disturbing dream she disliked the

thought of her engagement and the marriage into which Uncle Silas was forcing her. She hung about the Club in an irritable frame of mind until Richard rang her up. Then she found herself questioning him eagerly about poor Tony; forgetting her grievances about the Richard of the dream.

'Sir Basil says the operation is a complete success, and that he hopes Tony will be walking about as strong as a horse by August,' Richard told her, a deep note of thankfulness in his voice.

She said:

'Oh, I'm glad—frightfully glad, Richard.'

'It's such a relief, having it over,' he said. 'I've seen the lad. He's weak and in some pain, but wonderfully cheery and bucked about things.'

'Now you must stop being anxious, and come round and have a drink,' she said, with her usual generosity.

He came round within twenty minutes and sat in the Club talking to her, making plans for the future. He was to remain in town near Tony until he was much stronger. Graham wanted him to stay in the nursing-home for at least six weeks.

'That's all right,' said Billie. 'I shall go home this evening and see about closing up the bungalow for a bit, then Vera and I can stay here and we'll be on the spot when my uncle arrives.'

Richard felt a sudden small shock.

'The uncle! Oh, lord, yes—when is he due?'

'The end of next week,' said Billie, grimacing. 'And then, friend Richard, we shall be plunged into matrimony.'

Richard raised his cocktail glass.

'Good luck,' he said solemnly.

CHAPTER 10

ON the morning of Uncle Silas's arrival in London, Billie admitted to Vera that the first meeting with him and the introduction of her prospective husband were going to be nerve-racking.

'Uncle Silas is a sentimental old fool and will insist upon sob-stuff, and I just can't cope with it!' she told Vera, who was sitting on the edge of an armchair in Billie's bedroom at the Club.

Vera puffed daintily at a cigarette, and regarded the burning end reflectively.

'Oh, I dare say things will go off all right, my dear,' she said. 'What does Richard feel about it?'

'He's as nervy as I am,' said Billie, with a short laugh. 'It's a difficult situation.'

'I can't think why you don't fall in love with each other and have done with it,' said Vera.

Billie crushed a black felt hat down on her cropped head, and snorted with indignation at Vera's reflection in the mirror. Her temper was not of the best to-day. It was hot and sultry in town. Billie loathed town; longed for the country, because it was June and the time for green fields and blue sea and the wide untrammelled spaces. She was dreading the next few hours—Uncle Silas cross-examining her, cross-examining Richard—the stifling atmosphere of the hotel, where at his cabled command she had booked a suite for him. And there would be a celebration dinner to-night, without doubt.

'Don't talk to me about love!' she snapped. 'I assure you,

my dear V., I'd give half my money for you to be in my shoes.'

'I wish I were,' muttered Vera to herself.

Vera had seen Richard once or twice this week—dined with him and Billie, accompanied them to the nursing-home to see Tony. And the more Vera saw of Richard, the more she admired him. She was, in fact, fast developing one of her frequent 'passions.' If Vera was not in love with one man, she was with another. It was only because she possessed a mercenary little mind and intended to wait for a man with money that she was not already married. Richard was poor, but Richard was very handsome and attractive and completely indifferent to her, therefore she was bound to fall in love with him. Let Billie marry him—oh yes! and keep the fortune Vera found so useful—let her maintain this cold, platonic attitude ... oh yes! But later, Vera would have her chance with Richard. Vera knew much more about men than Billie, and one day in the future, when Richard was lonely and bored ...

'Uncle Silas will be at the Ritz at three o'clock, so I shall have to dash off to him now,' said Billie, interrupting Vera's amorous reflections. 'Thank goodness he'll have to include you in the celebration dinner to-night. You can help me out.'

'How? By flirting with Richard?' asked Vera, with a wicked gleam in the blue eyes which looked so round and innocent.

'No,' said Billie angrily. 'By helping us to make my wretched uncle believe this to be a love-match, you little idiot.'

'Right you are,' said Vera, unruffled. 'I'll whisper to him in the course of the evening that never have I known a more exquisite modern case of Romeo and Juliet than you and your Richard.'

Completely sickened, Billie marched out of the bedroom, hands boyishly thrust in her coat-pockets, mouth tightly shut. She felt wrapped in gloom as she drove in a taxi through the sunlit streets to the Ritz. She was too frank and natural fundamentally to lie or deceive with Vera's ease. She

58

cordially dreaded her meeting with her uncle. But she tried to think of the money—the fortune she would forfeit unless she carried her scheme through.

Then there was Tony; Billie always softened at the memory of the crippled boy to whom her money had been so invaluable. He was now on the high road to recovery—one of Sir Basil Graham's most successful cases. Every day he was growing stronger, nearer to the time when he would be able to rise from his sick-bed and learn to walk again.,

Billie and Richard were good friends. They understood each other. That was some consolation. And she could not help but admire him. He took no more money from her than he could possibly help, and he was writing—she knew he spent most of his leisure time on a book which he had commenced—was working at it when not able to be with his young brother. Richard's one wish now was to make money for himself—to repay the girl to whom he was already heavily in debt.

Billie's lips curved into a faint smile at the thought of him.

'Poor thing!—he's as terrified as I am of our approaching marriage,' she reflected grimly. 'Fall in love! No, I'll leave that sort of emotional stuff to V. Richard and I don't believe in it.'

Ten minutes later she was in the flower-scented, sumptuous sitting-room of Silas G. Carden's suite at the Ritz, being hugged, flattered, and congratulated—all of which she suffered, feeling one of this life's martyrs.

'Gee, if this isn't real great to come over and find my little gurl niece engaged to be married!' Mr. Carden enthused, now holding her at arm's length and regarding her with genuine affection. 'Say, how lovely you're looking, Billie Carden! I always said Silas G. Carden's niece and heiress would turn into a real beauty, and she has!'

'Oh, rot!' said Billie, scarlet and uncomfortable.

He examined her left hand.,

'Why, yes, there's the ring. My! a nice little pearl. Tell me all about your sweetheart, honey. Got any money?'

'No—not a penny.'

59

'That don't matter if you care for him. You've got plenty for two. I'll settle a bit on him if I like him. Crazy about him, are you?'

'Oh yes,' muttered Billie, burying her nose in a bunch of pink roses which stood on the centre table.

'Wall, he's sure to be just mad over you, honey, eh?'

'Oh yes,' repeated Billie, with cheeks as pink as the roses, and heart thumping.

The expected bombardment of questions continued. Mr. Carden wished to know where she had met him, what his profession was, who his relatives were, where he lived. Some of her answers seemed to disappoint him, but on the whole he appeared satisfied.

'I reckon my niece might have married a Dook; but if you're crazy over this chap, why I'm not going to sniff at him,' he announced cheerfully. 'As for him having divorced his first wife, why, that's common enough over our side of the herring-pond; but I don't approve of divorce, so mind you stick to him, honey.'

Billie stared at her uncle in silence. He always reduced her to speechlessness. An overwhelming personality was Silas G. Carden, whose god was money, and whom money had made a god. When he gave, he gave generously, but expected his wishes and desires to be carried out. He was a wilful man. If his niece had not obeyed his command, and decided to marry and settle down, he would undoubtedly have disinherited her. He was very fond of her, proud of her good looks and her sharp brains. He had hitherto been content to let her live in England with her cousin, Vera Disney, and to allow her two thousand a year and freedom. He himself lived a busy life, necessitating much travel in the States, and had not wanted his heiress to live with him. But he did not approve of the attitude she had recently adopted toward men. He disliked masculine women and theories against marriage and children. It delighted him to think that Billie had found a man she could marry, and with whom she could be happy.

Now it only remained for him to meet that man and approve of the match.

Silas G. Carden loved romance with a capital R. He had in his youth loved and married a woman to whom he had been faithful till the day she had died. It had been a bitter disappointment that there had been no child of the union. Upon Billie, his brother's daughter, he placed his hopes. And one of his most earnest desires was to see her happily married with a family of her own, before he died and the Carden fortune should pass out of his hands into hers.

Richard arrived at the Ritz, was shown up to the Carden suite, and found Billie sitting by an open window, smoking and listening to a short, stout little man with a huge mass of curly iron-grey hair, who was walking excitedly up and down the room, expounding his theories upon love.

'Nothin' like it in the world, my gurl!' he was saying, when Richard entered the room. 'You can say what you like about freedom and independence, but the happiest hours of my life were spent with your Aunt Sally—bless her memory!—and I remember on our honeymoon way down in Pasadena . . .'

'Mr. Bromley!' squeaked a minute page-boy, who ushered Richard in. Uncle Silas stopped in the middle of his sentimental reflections (much to Billie's relief—Billie had listened too often to tales of Aunt Sally on that honeymoon), swung round, and regarded his future nephew-in-law, the all-important man who was to marry his heiress.

For a moment Richard stood rather stiffly at attention, as though under inspection from an Army General. He, like most people, became very speedily conscious of the personality and power of the stout, shaggy-haired little man who stared at him with keen, twinkling eyes, cigar at the corner of his mouth, thumbs in his yellow waistcoat.

Then Billie rose to the occasion and came forward, clearing her throat.

'Uncle Silas—my—my fiancé,' she said. 'Richard, this is my uncle, Mr. Carden.'

'How-do-you-do? stammered Richard more nervous than

he had ever been on Active Service in France.

'I'm pleased to meet you, my boy,' said Mr. Carden, taking the cigar from his mouth with one hand and gripping Richard's outstretched hand with the other. 'Pleased to meet you. So you're the chap who's stolen the heart of my little gurl, eh?'

Richard's handsome eyes met Billie's. Just for an instant they exchanged a glance of mutual sympathy and some amusement. Then the girl whose 'heart had been stolen' gave a helpless little giggle and turned away.

Mr. Carden's keen grey eyes took stock of Richard. The young man's appearance pleased him. He appreciated plenty of sinew and muscle; liked the broad shoulders and slim hips and lean brown face of Billie's sweetheart. Good-looker all right, he reflected; clean cut, healthy—easy to see he was a sportsman—and Uncle Silas had a soft spot in his heart for the British sportsman. Yes, he liked the look of Richard Bromley, and any fears he might have entertained that Billie had chosen a fop or a fool were satisfactorily swept away.

'Sit down, sit down, my boy,' he said, waving Richard to a chair. 'Have a cigar.'

Richard refused the cigar, but lit a cigarette. He first of all mopped his forehead with his handkerchief. It might have been the heat—for he had walked from Wimpole Street to the Ritz—or nervousness—or both. But he avoided Billie's eye, and centred his gaze studiously upon Silas Carden.

'Great thing for me to come over the herring-pond and find Billie with a sweetheart,' Mr. Carden was saying. 'It's always been my great wish to see her tied up to the right man. Mark you, she's a wilful girl, is Billie. I know her. You'll find her a bit of a handful, no doubt. Ha! ha!'

He roared. Richard laughed politely and coldly with him. Billie stared at nothing. Mr. Carden gave a sly glance from one to another. Yes, he loved a romance. And here were an engaged couple, no doubt a little shy and coy because the old uncle was present. A goodly pair to look at. It warmed the cockles of Silas G. Carden's heart. Pretty Billie, with her chestnut head and greeny eyes and fine, pale skin—and this black-haired, blue-eyed giant of hers.

'Don't mind me, you two, he said, beaming at them. 'All the world loves a lover, and so do I. Say, Richard Bromley, give her a kiss. I bet she's waiting for it.'

'Oh, rot!' began Billie hurriedly, with scarlet cheeks. The sensation of a trapped creature was stealing over her. She felt almost inclined in this moment to be rude to her uncle, throw up the fortune, and march out of the room. She only refrained because she felt it would be weak to give in at the first difficulty—and she hated giving in to anything, anyhow.

'Now, now, I don't mind, and you mustn't mind me,' said Uncle Silas heartily. 'Go and kiss her, my boy.'

Richard, agonised, looked with appealing eyes at Billie. She gave an almost imperceptible shrug of slim shoulders. It seemed to him that she felt, as he did—it would appear strange to Mr. Carden if they failed to respond to his invitation.

He rose and walked to Billie's side.

'I'm sorry,' he whispered. 'I suppose I must.'

'Yes—get it over,' she muttered.

With the knowledge that Uncle Silas's eagle eye regarded them from the other end of the room, Richard put an arm around the girl's shoulders, bent down, and kissed her. He was so nervous that he did not quite know where the kiss fell—it was somewhere between the corner of her mouth and her cheek. At any rate, it was a very fleeting kiss, and with no emotion behind it whatsoever. But it was just long enough for Richard to catch the subtle fragrance of her hair, and to feel the amazing softness of that mouth which looked boyish and hard.

He drew back, surprised and a little baffled to find his heart pounding as though he were an awkward lad kissing a girl for the first time in his life—he, Richard Bromley, once a married man—he, whom Olive had once called her 'loveliest lover on earth.'

Stung by memories, and annoyed with himself for letting that light kiss so disturb him, Richard marched away from Billie, and dived into his pocket for another cigarette. She meanwhile had sat quite motionless duing the embrace, her own nerves tingling, her cheeks hot and scarlet. It was the first time in Billie's life that she had been kissed by any man save her father and uncle. But if the fleeting caress from Richard had disturbed her, she was the first to recover her equilibrium. She saw how dangerous it would be to permit this atmosphere of drama to remain. Uncle Silas would soon notice it. She suddenly rippled with laughter.

'Now, Uncle Silas, are you satisfied?' she asked satirically.

'I wouldn't have called that much of a kiss in my youth,' announced Mr. Carden. 'Neither would your Aunt Sally. Now I remember, back in Pasadena——'

Richard and Billie were treated to a long and detailed account of that honeymoon which Silas G. Carden remembered with such tenderness. He even rushed into his bedroom to fetch a photograph of the deceased Aunt Sally to show Richard. Once he had vanished, Richard walked quickly to Billie's side.

'I say—I'm sorry about that. But I—er—had to,' he stammered.

She met his gaze quite coolly and carelessly now.

'Oh, don't worry. It's all in the day's work. I didn't take any notice of it, my dear Richard,' she said.

'That's all right, then,' he said a trifle stiffly.

And again Richard surprised himself by feeling almost hurt that she should have taken no notice of his caress. Cold-blooded little devil, this Billie! Well, did he wish her to be otherwise?

'I'm a complete fool,' Richard told himself savagely. 'This was a stone-cold compact, and if I'm going to forget that and lose my sense of humour, I'd better back out of the engagement now—this very minute!'

But Richard did not back out of the engagement. Having cursed himself for a fool, he recovered the sense of humour which he had been on the point of losing, and began to see what a humorous situation it was, after all. He listened to Mr. Carden's rhapsodies on his late wife, admired Aunt Sally's photograph, then Billie made her exit.

'You two might want a little chat,' she said. 'I'll see you later, Uncle Silas.'

'Sure, honey,' he beamed at her. 'What about a little dinner here at the Ritz to-night, to celebrate the engagement? Bring your pretty cousin Vera right along, too.'

'Thanks awfully,' said Billie.

She threw a hasty smile at Richard.

'See you later, old thing,' she said, and rapidly vanished before her terrible uncle could suggest another lover's embrace.

CHAPTER 11

MR. CARDEN hunched his shoulders. 'Say, boy, I'm mighty glad Sally never called me "old thing,"' he confided. 'It's a term of endearment I just can't appreciate.'

Richard smiled. He knew quite well that Billie had flung that 'old thing' at him for the uncle's benefit. It had come more easily from her than 'darling' or 'dearest.'

Then he found himself plunged by Mr. Carden into the business side of the engagement.

'You've no money—Billie told me that—but I don't mind. I like you, boy and I'm willing to settle a bit on you the day you marry my little girl.'

Richard, rather red in the face, thanked him

'I can't say I like taking it,' he blurted out. 'It's more than kind of you, Mr. Carden. But I'm writing a book, and if it goes, I shall be able to repay you a little, I hope, and——'

'Cut that right out, boy,' interrupted Uncle Silas. 'I like your spirit, but I don't want you to repay me. I'm a rich man, and I can afford to give away a few thousand dollars. All I really want is to see that little gurl happy. If you love her and promise me to be good to her, that's enough for Silas G. Carden.'

Richard choked a bit over that promise. It was exceedingly difficult to play his part with skill and finish to the last ounce. It seemed such a rotten farce to him to be swearing to love and cherish a girl who intended to live her own life as soon as Mr. Carden departed to America again. It was only the memory of the boy in Sir Basil Graham's nursing-home—of the wonderful chances that were being given him through this affair with Billie—which pulled Richard successfully through that difficult hour with Silas G. Carden.

At the end of it, Mr. Carden had decided to settle a sum that seemed to Richard altogether excessive upon his niece's husband on the day of their marriage.

'And say, I want that marriage to take place mighty soon, before I go back to Noo York,' Uncle Silas announced. 'You two'd better fix up the date to-night, eh?'

'Yes,' said Richard. 'I'll ask Billie.'

He left the Ritz in a state of gloom. All this money and talk of money depressed him. It was not that he disliked spending it. He was as fond of the good things of this world as any ordinary young man. But he hated taking it for nothing.

'I suppose Billie would call me a damn fool, and remind me that I'm discharging the debt by marrying her,' he reflected. 'But if it weren't for old Tony, I'd chuck it. It worries me.'

Billie returned to her Club equally depressed and worried. She poured out her woes to Vera before they dressed for the dreaded celebration dinner.

'I'm so fed up, I'm beginning to wish I'd defied Uncle Silas and refused to marry,' she said, her grey-green eyes mutinous. 'It's the hardest thing on earth to me to play up to

Richard and pretend I'm in love with him.'

Vera hastened to console her.

'Remember all you'd lose if you didn't carry this through, Bill,' she said. 'No Vauxhall, no racer, no bungalow, no Club—nothing!'

'H'm,' said Billie, gloomily sipping a cocktail. 'Well, I suppose it's got to be done. I should hate to be poor. Richard isn't enjoying himself any more than I am.'

Suddenly her hand went up to her cheek. She dug one slim finger into the spot where Richard's kiss had fallen, and found herself blushing furiously.

'It's all such rot,' she muttered. 'What is love? Why all this fuss about marrying for love? It makes me sick.'

'Don't you know your Shakespeare?' murmured Vera:

> '"What is love? Tis not hereafter;
> Present mirth hath present laughter,
>   What's to come is still unsure;
> In delay there lies no plenty;
> Then come kiss me, sweet-and-twenty!
>   Youth's a stuff will not endure."'

Billie set down her cocktail glass and rose to her feet, yawning.

'That suits you nicely, V.' she said. 'But I'd rather go to the British Museum with Richard and improve my mind than sit in a room with artistically lowered lights and be kissed. I'm going up to dress. Coming?'

'Yes. You're a hopeless case,' said Vera, sighing.

The happiest couple at the celebration dinner were undoubtedly Uncle Silas and Vera. The former beamed at his little party, drank the healths of the engaged couple in the best dry champagne, and congratulated himself that his niece was marrying a really good fellow. Vera always expanded like a flower in the sun to the festive atmosphere of a smart London restaurant. She looked exceedingly pretty in a pink and silver frock, flirted her big blue eyes at Richard (who stonily disregarded her and interested himself in his food), and enjoyed herself to the best of her ability. She certainly helped the situation by keeping up a flow of light, frivolous chatter, and Uncle Silas thought her a 'dear little thing.'

Billie was ill at ease the whole evening. For her uncle's benefit she wore a more festive and feminine frock than usual. It was pale sea-green, rather straight and tight to the hips, then fluted and full, falling just below the knee. It made her eyes looked brilliantly green beneath their thick dark lashes, and the heat of the room had brought a slight colour to her cheeks. She looked lovely to-night, but she was unconscious of her allure, and felt like a fish out of water.

Before the celebration dinner had ended, Uncle Silas brought the conversation round to the forth-coming wedding-day.

'I must get way back to Noo York by the end of the month,' he said. 'Say, what about you two young folk getting married the middle of the month—say the fifteenth or sixteenth of June?'

Billie's heart missed a beat. She caught Richard's gaze. Then she lowered her lashes nervously.

'Oh yes, all right—I don't mind,' she said. 'Only—er-it's a very short engagement.'

'What's that matter, when you're in love?' said Mr. Carden sentimentally. 'The sooner the better. Richard, my boy, will you fix things up for round about the middle of June?'

'Yes, if—if Billie is willing,' said Richard.

'Quite,' said Billie, clearing her throat.

'Where will you spend the honeymoon?' asked Mr. Carden.

Richard, the coward, left Billie to answer the awkward question. Vera looked on with amusement.

'Oh, er—we really haven't discussed it,' stammered Billie.

'Then I'll fix it up,' said Uncle Silas. 'You just leave things to me.'

Billie bit her under lip. Uncle Silas was most difficult. Heaven only knew what he might arrange. She wished heartily that he would return to New York to-morrow and leave them all alone.

The rest of the evening passed with fair success. Vera wanted to dance, but to Billie's relief Richard announced that he was not a dancing man, so Mr. Carden took them on to a revue. At midnight Richard was left to see the two girls back to the Club. Vera stepped out of the taxi first, and discreetly left the other two alone.

Richard looked down at Billie. She seemed pale and tired.

'My dear girl, I'm afraid this is all going to be too much for you,' he said. 'You look fagged out to-night.'

'Oh, I'm all right,' she said shortly. 'But Uncle Silas would sap anybody's vitality. One can't relax for a moment with him.'

'We've played our parts well, haven't we?' asked Richard, with a wry smile. 'He thinks us fond lovers, doesn't he?'

'Yes,' she nodded. 'But the strain will come in keeping up the appearance. I'm sorry for you, friend Richard.'

'Why?'

'Oh, I'm an ill-tempered little pig, and Vera says I'm quite unnatural. It's a pity you aren't going to marry her.'

'Is it? Well, I don't think so,' said Richard quite huffily. 'I couldn't begin to manage a blue-eyed, golden-haired pet like Miss Vera.'

That made Billie smile, and she was secretly pleased that he preferred her. She was human enough to possess a little vanity.

'Well, good-night, Richard,' she said. 'And I suppose we must see it through. Fix the wedding for the fifteenth, if you like. I refuse to be a bride in a trailing gown, with a misty veil and all that rot. It's a registry office for me. I'll tell Uncle Silas I prefer it.'

'Right,' said Richard. 'And I infinitely prefer it. But, Billie, I say, what on earth does the old man mean to arrange for our honeymoon?'

'Gawd knows!' said Billie irreverently. 'But let him have his own way. We'll baffle him somehow, whatever awful idea he fixes.'

They parted good friends.

Billie went to sleep thinking of Richard with something approaching affection.

'He's a good sort,' she reflected drowsily. 'I needn't worry about him. He'll always play the game.'

CHAPTER 12

DURING the next two weeks Billie found herself perforce doing the one thing that least interested her—buying clothes. Uncle Silas insisted upon presenting her with a huge cheque for her trousseau. She had to make some pretence of gathering one together. Vera thoroughly enjoyed herself making purchases on her cousin's behalf. So Billie—secretly chafing for her bungalow, for the sweep of the Sussex Downs, for a car to tinker with—was surrounded by foamy frocks, dozens of pairs of cob-webby silk stockings, hats and shoes and gloves—things she never intended to wear, but which would come in for Vera once Uncle Silas departed.

The dreaded wedding-day came much sooner than it was expected. It seemed to Billie that all of a sudden she went to sleep, then woke up to find it was 15th June. Richard had made all the arrangements. They were to be married at half-past twelve at the Marylebone Registry Office. He had bought the ring and she had already tried it on, defying superstition. There was no drawing back for them now.

Uncle Silas was as excited as a child about it all. He regretted that his beautiful niecé and heiress refused to have a full and fashionable wedding at St. George's, Hanover Square. Registry-office weddings seemed to him dull and unromantic. However, he had respected the wish of the young pair. The affair was to be quiet, with just himself and

Vera as witnesses. And after the wedding he was going to give them a surprise, along with that fat cheque to Richard.

'I've fixed your honeymoon up for you,' he had told them on the wedding eve. 'I won't tell you about it now, but you'll like my plans, I know.'

Needless to say, both Richard and Billie were in a state of suspense.

It would be difficult to say whether the bride or bridegroom was the most nervous on 15th June. Richard dressed himself in a new grey suit, hastily made for him by his old tailors, who had delightedly welcomed him back to their expensive fold; then went round to the nursing-home to see his brother.

Tony was quite excited and enthusiastic about the wedding.

'I do wish I could have come, Dick,' he said. 'I expect Billie will look sweet. She's such a dear, isn't she?'

'She's been damn good to us, Tony,' muttered Richard.

'How does it feel to be a prospective bridegroom?' Tony laughed.

Richard echoed the laugh very nervously.

'Oh, I don't know, old chap.'

'But you're very much in love—you're going to be happy this time, aren't you, Dick?' asked the boy more seriously.

Richard failed to answer for a moment. His emotions were altogether chaotic this morning. He could hardly realise that he was about to make Billie Carden his wife. Yet the ring lay in his vest-pocket—waiting; and soon she would be with her uncle and Vera at the registry office, waiting . . .

Instinctively his mind leaped back to the day of his marriage with Olive. What years ago it seemed!—yet it was so short a while . . . what a buoyant, happy-go-lucky, radiant bridegroom he had been that day! . . . the proper bridegroom, in a frock-coat and silk hat . . . and Olive a pretty, blushing bride . . . at St. Peter's Church, in Eastbourne, which had been her home. That day he had believed in love . . . believed in Olive. She had promised to love, honour, and obey ... then let him down.

This wedding-day was so different. Billie was to make no promises—so could break none. It was just an empty form ... a mercenary contract. And Tony had said: 'You're going to be happy *this time*, aren't you, Dick?'

He felt suddenly miserable, almost ashamed to face his young brother.

'I must get along now, old chap,' he said. 'So long. We'll come and see you—afterwards.'

Tony wrung his hand.

'Good-bye. Good luck, Dick, and give my love to Billie.'

At this precise moment a very pale, nerve-racked Billie left the Club with her uncle and cousin, stepped into the Daimler limousine which Mr. Carden had hired for the occasion, and was driven to Marylebone.

There was no denying that Vera looked like the bride. She was exquisite, radiant in a powder-blue georgette gown, with a big black picture hat on her golden head. Vera was quite happy. She felt in this hour that her own fortunes were secure. Billie would retain the Carden money now, and once Uncle Silas had gone, she, Vera, was temporarily to live with the married pair in the rôle of chaperon. That was excellent. Vera very much wanted to see a good deal of Richard.

Billie's expression was that of a martyr, and not a very heroic one. She was pale—grim. She knew in her heart that Richard was not going to make any difference to her life, and yet she felt she was losing her freedom and independence just by losing her maiden name. In an hour's time she would no longer be Billie Carden. She would be Mrs. Richard Bromley. Incredible fact!

She was more soberly dressed than Vera. She had chosen a stone-grey frock of pleated georgette, and wore a small grey hat on her boyish brown head. Grey shoes and silver stockings, and a beautiful light sable stole completed a charming, chic toilette. But although it altered her personality from outward appearances, and made a smart young woman of her, she was inwardly the old Billie—the same blunt, boyish Billie. And she went to this wedding with the sensation of one going to a funeral.

Uncle Silas, resplendent in grey bowler and spats, a white rose in his buttonhole, had given his niece a string of pearls and a gorgeous bunch of June roses and lilies-of-the-valley when he had met her. She put on the pearls, but begged to be allowed to leave the flowers at her Club.

'I'll wear one or two,' she said, to mollify the old man, and hastily pinned two roses on her shoulder. 'But I can't bear a bridal bouquet, and letting the whole world know I'm a bride.'

'You young women to-day have no sentiment,' said Mr. Carden. 'Now your Aunt Sally——'

Tales of Aunt Sally revived Billie's drooping spirits all the way to the registry office.

Her heart thumped hard as she walked in on her uncle's arm, and saw Richard waiting for her in the little dusty, sunless room. Outside it was a hot, cloudless day of June. In the registry office it was dark and cheerless. Billie suddenly began to tremble. She saw Richard's face, very grim and resolute and rather white, like her own, and knew his own nerves were not very steady.

'I can't think why I ever began this business,' she told herself helplessly. 'It's too awful ...'

Richard gave one swift look at her. It was indeed very different from that wedding of years ago. There was no sentiment in it, no wild, rapturous hopes, no passionate believe in life or love, no heart-burnings or sharp secret thrills. It was cold, cut and dried, rather meaningless. Yet this slender girl in grey, with her sable stole, her exquisite pearls, was not only an heiress, but a very attractive, intelligent, beautiful young woman. And she was to bear his name, Mrs. Bromley ... the name Olive had once borne, and then disgraced and discarded for another.

He suddenly found it impossible to be without any emotion of any sort. He could see that Billie, poor child, was shaking with nerves, and he knew exactly what she felt. On an impulse he walked up to her, and took both her hands.

'Buck up, my dear!' he whispered.

It was bluntly spoken, and the strong pressure of his fingers was purely friendly. Billie responded to both. She looked up into the man's blue eyes, and found them encouraging and tender, instead of the hard, cynical eyes which had grown familiar. She felt a queer contraction of the throat.

'Lord, it's awful!' she whispered back, with a half-giggle. 'Being married's much worse than having a tooth out without gas. I hope I never get married again, Richard.'

'I hope you never do, but one never knows. Look at me. I swore I would never repeat the act.'

That reminded her suddenly of his unfortunate marriage. She forgot her own grievances, and patted his shoulder.

'Cheer up, friend Richard; I won't cause you to repent of this rash act. We understand each other.'

He found himself thrilling under the touch of her hand. Then the registrar, with a bland smile, asked them if they were ready—Richard fumbled in his pocket for the ring—and the all-important words were spoken ...

Vera, standing just behind Richard, stared at his dark, handsome head, and bitterly envied the girl at his side.

'How can she be so cool and unmoved? I'd be in a state of the wildest excitement,' she mused. 'He's so splendid!'

As though in a dream, Billie heard herself responding to the dry questions put to her by the registrar. She awoke with a shock when he shook her warmly by the hand, and said:

'Let me congratulate you, Mrs. Bromley.'

Mrs. Bromley! Heavens! How curious that sounded. Was it possible that she could never call herself Miss Carden again? She stared down at her marriage finger. Cynically she regarded the thin platinum circlet which Richard had just placed upon it. 'The mark of servitude,' she had once designated all wedding-rings. Well, this one was not a mark of servitude. She was not going to serve Richard, or any other man.

74

Uncle Silas's deep voice boomed out in the little office:

'Bless you both. Now then, Richard, my boy, you're sure going to kiss your little bride, ain't you?'

With a nervous laugh, Richard slid an arm around the girl who was now by law his wife.

'Here's luck,' he said.

She was no longer trembling. Cool and collected she received his light, brief kiss, then turned away with a high colour in her cheeks.

'Come along,' said Uncle Silas. 'I've arranged lunch for you at the Berkeley.'

Vera slid an arm through Billie's, and whispered in her ear:

'Well, darling, how does it feel to be a married woman?'

'Exactly the same as I felt before,' snapped Billie. 'And don't call me "darling." I hate it.'

CHAPTER 13

DURING luncheon at the Berkely, Uncle Silas exploded his bombshell about the honeymoon.

'Now I'll tell you my little surprise,' he said, beaming from bride to bridegroom. 'You neither of you seemed to mind where you went, so I guess I've fixed up something real nice. I've been busy this last week. That couple o' days I spent out of London, I was in Cornwall—down that wonderful Tintagel way, where the real romantic old King Arthur's Castle lies in ruins. And I saw a perfectly lovely house close by, to let furnished for six months, so I rented it for you. It's waiting to receive you—maids and all. I reckoned Mrs. Richard would motor down in her Vauxhall with her hubby, and that you could spend a real romantic honeymoon there, undisturbed. It's miles from any one, and ideal summer weather. A real fine historic house it is, called Gale Towers, and belongs to an old Cornish nobleman—Sir Percy Penhollis. Now then, young folk, are you pleased? and will you accept Gale Towers for your honeymoon?'

Billie and Richard exchanged glances. They were both frankly nonplussed, and aware that not only Uncle Silas's eye was steadily upon them, but that Vera was regarding them with a certain malicious amusement. She, who knew the compact between these two, was quite aware that they were being placed in an exceedingly awkward predicament.

How could they refuse Gale Towers? The old man had motored down to Cornwall expressly to find them a romantic house for the honeymoon, and had taken it. He left them no choice. But the last thing either of them wanted was seclusion amidst 'romantic surroundings.'

Uncle Silas rubbed his hands, and beamed from his niece to his newly made nephew.

'Say, babes, how does it strike you?' he drawled.

Richard smothered a groan. To be called 'Babe' was bad enough; to be forced into taking Billie down to Tintagel for a supposed honeymoon was worse. Generous though Uncle Silas had been in a financial way, Richard did not like him in this awkward hour.

Billie was left to respond to her uncle. With heightened colour and downcast lashes, she said:

'Thanks most awfully, Uncle. It—it's very decent of you indeed to—er—have done this.'

'Very decent,' echoed Richard, taking his cue.

'Then you like the plan?'

'Of course,' said Billie, clearing her throat and avoiding Vera's twinkling eye, whilst secretly kicking that young woman in a most un-bride-like fashion under the table.

'Ripping spot, Tintagel,' muttered Richard.

'You know it?' beamed Mr. Carden.

'Been down once, yes, when my brother was a bit of a kid. I remember my mother taking us to Trebarwith Strand. That's close by,' said Richard.

'Indeed? Wall, say, that's mighty good. Gale Towers is half-way between Tintagel Church and Trebarwith,' said Mr. Carden, his smile broadening. Cigar in his mouth and thumbs in his waistcoat, he regarded Richard with a satisfied air. 'You'll know the place—grey walls, turrets, sort of miniature castle in itself?'

'I fancy I know the place,' murmured Richard.

'Say, Billie gurl'—Mr. Carden turned to his niece—'my plan's all right, then? You'll take your husband right down in the automobile, eh?'

Billie hesitated for a moment, then resigned herself to fate. After all, once she and Richard got away from Uncle Silas, they could do more or less what they wanted—even though they were forced to go to this wretched Gale Towers.

'I wish a gale would blow up and hurl the place into the sea,' she thought, with a burst of childish anger. Aloud she said: 'Right you are, Uncle Silas.'

Mr. Carden examined his large gold watch.

'I reckon you'd better be starting then,' said he. 'It's a good long way down there.'

'We can't possibly get to Tintagel to-night,' said Richard. 'We'll have to break the journey.'

'Yes—at Exeter,' said Billie gloomily.

'That's just fine,' said Uncle Silas. 'It's one of your nice English cathedral towns, and you two honeymooners can wander round and see the views, then motor on to Tintagel in the morning.'

Vera stifled a laugh. Billie's face was a study. If one thing was anathema to Billie, it was a cathedral town. In silence the little party rose and retired to Mr. Carden's private sitting-room to say farewell.

Billie, left alone with her cousin for a moment dabbed some powder on her nose, pulled her hat low over her brow, then scowled at her refletion.

'I feel a sight!' she growled.

'You look sweet,' said Vera. 'Quite the bride in that grey get-up, with your pearls and your sable stole.'

'Bride, indeed!' snorted Billie.

'Well, aren't you one?' said Vera, enjoying herself.

'Not as you think of a bride,' said Billie, pulling the hat still lower over her forehead with a vicious little movement. 'I'm sick to death of Uncle Silas and his romantic temperament, and fed up with the whole affair.'

'Too late, darling,' purred Vera. 'You're married.'

Billie glanced at her left hand.

'I'm Mrs. Bromley by law, and that's as far as it goes,' she said.

'Poor Richard!' sighed Vera.

'What do you mean?' said Billie, her eyes snapping. 'Why "poor Richard"?'

Vera lowered her lashes and hummed under her breath.

'Oh, you don't know men as I know them, my dear,' she said evasively. 'But just wait—see if he continues to like this state of affairs. I wouldn't if I were he.'

'But you're not, and he is different from the infatuated fools you've met,' said Billie, with some heat. 'Good-bye, Vera. I hope you'll enjoy carting Uncle Silas about town till my *honeymoon* is ended.'

'I shall,' said Vera, laughing. 'And still more shall I enjoy coming to you later on, and seeing what a hash you've both made of things. However—ta-ta, old thing—good luck!'

Thoroughly rattled and slightly disturbed, Billie marched out of the room and joined her uncle and the man to whom she had been married under such extraordinary circumstances. Richard was waiting in the lounge, his suit-case beside him, his handsome face puckered as though he were not enjoying Uncle Silas's conversation. He looked at Billie as she came toward him. It was strange to him to think she was his wife.

'We'll pick up my luggage at the Club, Richard,' she said. 'Then we must go to say good-bye to Tony.'

'Yes, we mustn't forget Tony,' said Richard.

Unle Silas embraced his niece with fervour.

'It's been a real happiness to me, little gurl, to attend your wedding,' he said. 'Bless you both—long life and happiness. I like your bo' and I bet he'll kind of look after you all right. Don't worry over money. I've handed him a real nice cheque.'

'Yes,' muttered Richard, very red in the face. 'He's been wonderfully kind, Billie.' Then he added lamely, 'come along—er—darling.'

That almost made her laugh. She hurriedly climbed into the Vauxhall, which a chauffeur had brought round to the Ritz for her. Vera detained Richard a moment. She gave him both hands, which he had to take, and lifted her pretty baby face to his.

'You must look upon me as your cousin and friend now, Richard,' she murmured. 'I *do* hope you'll be happy. If at any time I can help, send for me, won't you?'

He was quite unaware that she was thrilling at the touch of his fingers; that already she was attempting to coquette, to cast her feminine toils about him. He was just embarrassed; dropped her hands, and muttered, 'Thanks awfully.' Then he took his seat in the car beside his wife.

Tony awaited his brother and sister-in-law in state—highly delighted and excited. He was in the first stage of the cure, sitting up in a chair. It was not for years that poor Tony had sat upright, and it was a glorious, exhilarating feeling to him. He sat by the window overlooking Wimpole Street, in a grand blue dressing-gown embroidered with Chinese dragons (one of the generous Billie's gifts)—an enormous bunch of roses in his hands. The nurse in charge had brought the roses on his behalf.

'I haven't a brass farthing and I can't give Mrs. Bromley a decent present, so I shall buy her flowers,' he had said.

When Billie, followed by Richard, entered the room and saw the lad there, awaiting her with a smile of real affection on his thin sweet face, and the bouquet of pale pink roses in his hands, a lump rose to her throat. Speechlessly she put an arm about his neck and kissed him. It took a lot to make Billie kiss anybody! She was rewarded by a hug from the boy and a warm kiss in response.

'Ever so many congratulations, Billie,' he said huskily. 'I

do so hope you and Dick'll be happy. You deserve to be. You've been absolutely ripping to me. You've given me a new lease of life. Look at me, sitting upright. And next week I shall be learning to walk!'

'Great baby!' said Billie, to hide her emotion.

With the roses in her hands she moved away to make place for Richard, who shook hands with his young brother and received his congratulations.

'By jingo!' said Tony, looking from one to the other. 'You both look no end smart—quite the bridal pair.'

'H'm,' said Richard, with a short laugh. 'Billie is chic, I admit. But me ... oh, well, it's the first new suit Cool and Hutchins have made me for the dickens of a time, and it's not so bad, I suppose.'

'I think it very well cut,' put in Billie, 'and that light shade of grey is your colour, Richard.'

'Thanks, my dear,' he said lightly. Secretly he liked her praise.   They stayed with the invalid for half an hour. Then Richard glanced at his watch.

'We'll never get to Exeter to-night!' he said. 'We've left it much too late.'

'Then we'll go as far as Bath,' said Billie. 'I can do that by seven o'clock. It's four now.'

'What!—London to Bath in three hours—never——!' began Richard.

'My dear Richard,' broke in Billie, raising a hand, 'you don't know me yet. It's just about a hundred miles, and in the Vauxhall I can average thirty-five miles an hour—especially as I know the road.'

'I can see that my wife is going to be the death of me,' said Richard grimly.

'What a thing to say on your wedding-day!' said Tony, grinning.

'It's nothing to what he'll be saying next week,' said Billie cheerfully. 'I haven't promised to love, honour, or obey him, Tony.'

'But I'll bet you'll do all three,' said the boy, this time with gravity.

Billie thought it decidedly time to depart. She could not bear any sentiment from Tony. It made the situation too strained, and she was unwilling to hurt him, since he was weaving a romance around his brother's marriage. They bade him good-bye and left him happy, waving to them from the window.

The Vauxhall glided out of London, bearing the newly wedded pair in front, their luggage at the back. They were as unlike the love-sick pair of Tony's and Uncle Silas's imagination as they could be. They remained silent until they were well out of the suburbs. Then, rushing down the sunlit road with the trees, the fields, the sweeping country about them, Billie felt more herself. She began to expand. She pulled up the car, took off her hat, shook back her hair, and drew a deep breath.

'Now I feel better!' were her first words. 'London, the Ritz, that registry office stifled me, Richard. Give me a cigarette, for lord's sake.'

He handed her one with a smile.

'Poor Billie!' he said dryly. 'I sympathise with you. I was fairly stifled myself. Now we're safe from the madding crowd.'

'I was shaking with nerves, me—Billie Car—I mean, Billie Bromley—*with nerves*—and I'm normally as cool as a cucumber. But being married is too frightful.'

'I apologise humbly for *having* to marry you,' he said, lighting a cigarette for himself.

She drove on, cigarette in her mouth, still hatless—the boyish, careless Billie he knew.

'I don't mind now,' she said. 'We understand each other and can drop all this "darling" and "long-to-be-alone" rot.'

''Pon my soul, you're a funny little devil,' he said, regarding her much as he would have regarded some weird phenomenon. 'You haven't an ounce of sentiment in your body.'

'Oh yes, I have—for the right time and right thing. I was nearly weeping when Tony gave me those roses. I knew he'd saved up his pocket-money for them. Those are the things that move me, Richard. But I've no use for the love-rot, and you know it.'

'I wonder if you'll always feel like that.'

'Always.'

'I wonder,' he repeated.

'Don't wonder!' she begged. 'And don't let's discuss it. We're married, perforce, and we neither of us appreciate our lawful union, so let's forget it. We've got to go to this Cornish house to satisfy my uncle, but we'll send for Tony as soon as he can travel, and for Vera, to relieve the loneliness.'

'I don't so much mind being alone with you,' he said. 'I'm beginning to find you quite a good sort of pal.'

'That's the first real compliment I've had from you, Richard. Yes, we'll be pals all right, and you know how I feel about this marriage, so I rely on you to handle all the difficult situations that may arise, with tact.'

'I won't let you down,' he said. 'Lord, what a funny life! A month ago I was wondering how to earn my bread and butter if my next story didn't sell, and here I am, married to an heiress, with the biggest cheque in my pocket I've ever dreamed of.'

'Good for you—it's honestly earned,' she smiled.

'That's as it may be. But I hope to sell my book, make a furore one day, and pay you back.'

'We won't bother about it to-day,' she said.

'For God's sake don't drive so fast!' he said suddenly. 'You're doing fifty, and it's too much for a girl——'

'Talk to me like that, and I'll lose my temper with you, friend Richard,' she said, tilting her chin.

The speedometer leapt to sixty-five. The thirty-ninety Vauxhall was going down a straight piece of road like the wind. Richard set his teeth, clung to the side of the car, and regarded Billie's set, sharp little profile with apprehension in his heart.

'What a girl!' he thought. 'What a wedding ... what a difference from the day I married Olive. I wonder if I'm going to altogether like being defied and ignored by the new

Mrs. Bromley? I wonder if I'm going to find it quite so easy to treat her like a boy now she's—my wife?'

CHAPTER 14

THEY reached the Grand Pump Room Hotel, in Bath, soon after seven o'clock. Billie grinned at Richard as she drove the Vauxhall into the garage.

'Now, what about it?' she said. 'Feel safe driving with me in future?'

'Oh, I dare say,' he said. 'You're a rattling good driver, Billie, but I don't approve of speed-merchants, all the same, and one day you'll get locked up.'

'I've had my licence endorsed twice,' she admitted.

'Then you ought to be ashamed of yourself, and now you're Mrs. Bromley, kindly be careful of my spotless reputation and unblemished name.'

She bowed to him with mock humility.

'I'll do my best, de-ear husband!'

He was forced to laugh. One fact was certain. His association with this girl had brought the sparkle of humour back into his life. He had been growing sour and irritable, living in the Storrington cottage with poor old Tony. After Olive's desertion and the divorce, he had lapsed into a morose frame of mind not good for any man. He felt a different being to-day. After all, it was pleasant to have money in his pocket, to be getting about the country in a topping car, with a cheerful, sensible companion like Billie. If he had had any qualms about the marriage and the acceptance of her terms, they suddenly vanished. He began to feel light-hearted about the whole affair.

'I'm longing for a bath and a drink,' he said. 'Aren't you?'

'Rather. I'm smothered in dust.'

'But it's been a glorious afternoon, and the sunsets at Bath are worth seeing,' he said.

'They are,' she agreed. 'I came here with Vera for a week, a year ago. I like old Bath. The Roman Baths and excavations are most interesting.'

They entered the vestibule of the hotel, a porter behind them carrying their luggage. Richard felt that an awkward moment had arrived, and Billie knew just what he was feeling. Before he could ask, she said quite quietly:

'Two single rooms, Richard. It won't look at all stupid. Hundreds of married couples occupy separate rooms nowadays.'

He reddened very slightly.

'Of course. I'll see to that.'

Billie stood back while he asked for the rooms. It was strange and unreal to her to be here in this hotel, allowing a man to do everything. She was so accustomed to being her own mistress, to the management of her own affairs. When she travelled about the country with Vera, it was she, Billie, who took the man's place, arranged things, paid for them. She regarded Richard's broad back with contemplative eyes. Her husband ... her husband ... this tall, good-looking man who was even now registering their names—Mr. and Mrs. Richard Bromley.

A pretty, fair-haired girl, already in evening-dress strolled up to the reception bureau to ask for her letters. Billie saw her glance at Richard, then glance again, as though interested. That made Billie more thoughtful than ever.

'She's admiring him,' she mused. 'Of course he *is* good-looking—much nicer to look at than most men one sees about. Any woman would like the hard, brown look of him, and that Irish combination of blue eyes and black hair.'

The fair young thing in the pink evening-gown moved away, still giving Richard the full benefit of long-lashed eyes. But he was unaware of her admiring scrutiny, and turned to Billie, smiling.

'That's done,' he said. 'Come on.'

She moved with him to the lift, suddenly proud of her possession of him. For the first time in her life she was conscious of that acute feminine arrogance which inflates the heart of a woman when she walks beside a man at whom other women look—in vain. It was a novel experience, and she liked it. She was maliciously pleased that the young thing in pink had admired Richard, and received no response, and was quite aware that the girl was now disappointedly watching Richard being taken up in the lift with another woman who was obviously his wife.

'What's making you smile so funnily?' Richard asked her.

'Only my thoughts,' she said, and was horrified to feel her cheeks growing red and hot.

'Now I wonder what she's thinking?' Richard asked himself.

He had been married before, yet even after his experience with Olive, he had not yet given up trying to solve man's most difficult puzzle—the workings of a woman's brain!

Dinner that night at the Grand Pump Room Hotel was quite a success. Richard, conscious of his newly acquired wealth, ordered a special meal and champagne.

'Must drink to the health of my bride!' he grinned at Billie. 'And I trust you'll drink to me.'

'Certainly,' said she, raising her glass.

He thought how attractive she looked—in a new frock, which was one of the trousseau—a dark, wine-coloured chiffon with velvet flowers on the hem. As usual, the smooth brown hair was brushed glossily back from her brow. There was an extra golden tan to her clear-cut face after the long drive in the summer sunshine this afternoon.

'She isn't pretty in the bread-and-butter-miss style nor an exotic vamp,' thought Richard. 'But she's the most beautiful girl in the room by a long shot.'

They raised their goblets of cool, bubbling Perrier-Jouet 17, and the glasses clinked. Solemnly Richard looked into his wife's eyes.

'Here's my affection, esteem, and friendship,' he said.

'Thanks, old thing,' she said abruptly, and drank hers down.

He felt more thrilled by that curt speech than he would have been by the most impassioned words from any other woman of his acquaintance. And she knew in the depths of her heart that the affection, the esteem, and the friendship of this man were things to be valued. A while ago she would have cynically sympathised with any woman who left her husband, whilst dubbing her a fool for taking on a new one. To-night she began to wonder why Richard's first wife had run away from him. The girl must have been a fool and rather a rotten one, at that. She had left him because he had lost his money—eloped with some rich Guardee. A low-down trick to play. Richard had loved her and been good to her.

Billie cut short her own reverie.

'I can't let myself change just because I like Richard Bromley,' she grimly told herself. 'I shall only create unhappiness for myself if I become soft. It's the hard and practical people who suffer the least.'

She laid her table-napkin down.

'Let's go out into the air, Richard,' she said. 'It's warm in here. We might take a stroll along the river.'

'Capital idea,' he said.

They wandered out of the hotel, smoking; he hatless in his dinner-jacket; she with a light coat over the wine chiffon gown.

It was a perfect night. The picturesque city of Bath was etherealised into a fairy city under the blaze of white moonlight. The grand old Abbey stood out like a dark enchanted castle against the starry sky. The river, silvered, beautiful, wound serenely through the flower-filled garden that had been built on its banks. In the distance the beautiful Somerset hills dreamed darkly under the moon.

For a moment Richard and Billie stood silent, motionless, gazing around them. The sheer loveliness of the night put a spell upon them both.

The spell was broken by the deep tenor bell from Bath Abbey, sounding the hour of nine o'clock. Billie drew a long breath, and turned to her companion:

'Lovely, isn't it?' she said.

'One of the loveliest nights I've ever known,' he said.

She let her gaze rest on the river, threading its way like a wide silver ribbon between its green banks. Then she looked beyond to the enchanted hills, the indigo blue of the sky, with its myriad twinkling eyes. And she thought:

'My wedding night! How strange! I feel so cool, so calm, so unconcerned—because my marriage with this man is a mere formula—a farce. But if I had been in love with him, as Vera understands love—if I were really and truly a bride, at the side of her bridegroom this night of stars and magic, how different everything would be!'

Then she laughed at her own thoughts.

'Heaven forbid that I should indulge in the ecstasies of love!' she added to herself. 'What is love? A phantom—a will-o'-the-wisp—a maze in which one might get lost and starve, never find the way out again.'

'A penny for your thoughts, Billie,' said Richard's quiet voice from beside her.

She turned the collar of her coat up about her ears, and smoothed back a lock of hair which the night breeze had blown about her eyes.

'Not worth buying, my dear,' she said lightly. 'I was indulging in one of my cynical contemplations upon love.'

'Love!' echoed Richard. 'Oh, well, perhaps you are thinking, like I am, that we are a queer pair to be so utterly without emotion here under the stars, wrapped in beauty and solitude—and this our wedding night!'

Her straight brows met in a frown. She was not going to confess it was exactly that which she had been thinking. It struck her that the subject was too dangerous to be pursued. She found herself recollecting her dream of some nights ago ... the dream in which she had been caught to this man's heart, held passionately in his arms, her lips crushed beneath his mouth. The remembrance terrified her. In consequence she grew almost rude and curt with him.

'Oh, for lord's sake, Richard, let's stop talking of stars and solitude, and don't remind me of the unpleasant fact that we're married!' she exclaimed.

He flushed now. The sudden antagonism in her manner hurt him more than he cared to admit. He shrugged his shoulders.

'I've no wish to remind you of the fact,' he said stiffly. 'Shall we walk on?'

They moved along in silence. Neither spoke again until they returned to the hotel. Billie knew she had been rude, but could not bring herself to apologise. She became dumb on occasions when she felt herself to be in the wrong. Richard was nice, kind, considerate. Just because she had had a foolish dream, and was terrified of giving way to the least bit of sentiment, why be unkind to him? It was not his fault.

In the lounge he politely asked her to have a drink.

'No, thanks,' she said. 'I'm a bit tired. I'll run up to bed.'

'Right,' he said. 'Good-night.'

She hesitated. What she actually wanted to do was to shake hands with him and say, 'Don't mind me when I'm a little beast—I can't help it—I like you—I rely on you.' She remained silent, stammered a good-night, then fled from him.

He sat down in a chair in the crowded lounge, looking about him gloomily while he lit a cigarette and ordered a whisky-and-soda. He was struck by the dullness and ugliness of all the people about him. Fat, pompous old men, reading their newspapers, obviously here to take the 'baths.' Old ladies, covered with gold chains, bangles, brooches, and virtue, knitting in their corners. One or two married couples sitting beside each other, staring blankly before them. The usual stiff, conventional, unfriendly atmosphere of a British hotel lounge. Richard drank his whisky, and became gloomier every moment. He failed to understand why Billie had been so rude, had become so abrupt. She had been so charming at dinner. He failed to understand why he had been such a fool as to marry any girl on such a footing; he failed to understand himself, why he was hurt or annoyed by her attitude when he had himself renounced love or anything appertaining to it.

'Nobody in this world knows what they want, and when they get it they don't want it; and if they don't get it, they *do* want it,' he muttered, gulping down his drink.

With this, he set the glass on the table and lapsed into further gloom.

He thought of the girl he had married this morning, and who was upstairs now in her own room. He felt that there was an impenetrable wall between them. But he had agreed to that wall, so what right had he to resent it? No right at all. But to go down to Tintagel to-morrow, to carry on with the stars, the solitude, the supposed honeymoon, and retain a sense of humour, was going to be difficult.

He finally went to his bedroom, firmly convinced that he was a fool.

CHAPTER 15

SO passed the wedding night of Billie and Richard.

In the morning they met without any trace of antagonism—reasonable, healthy people—good friends, with good appetites. After a hearty breakfast they set forth in the Vauxhall for the cornish coast. By the time they got down there Billie had grown used to the wedding-ring on her slender finger; to being called 'Madam,' and thought of as Mrs. Richard Bromley. It did not seem to make any difference to her.

The next difficulties presented themselves at Gale Towers in Tintagel.

They had been struck by the beauty of Bath last night. The splendour of Gale Towers, which lay between Tintagel and Trebarwith Strand, enraptured them. They drove down a long, winding road past old, disused quarries, just as the sun was setting. Billie put on the brakes and sat still a moment.

'Look!' she said in a hushed voice.

Richard shaded his eyes with his hand, and stared down the deep valley to the sea. It lay like blue glass under a marvellous sky—rose, violet, vermilion, and blue—as the great red ball of the sun dipped deeper and deeper into the water, on the far horizon. Below the hill was Trebarwith Strand; a mile out stood the Gull Rock, around which the grey birds circled and screamed plaintively. The sea was very calm for the Cornish coast, and rippled lazily on to the golden sands. To the right lay Tintagel. They could just see the jagged ruins of King Arthur's castle silhouetted against the sunset sky.

Finally they moved on and came to Gale Towers, which stood right on the edge of the cliffs—a noble old building of rough-hewn stone, mellowed by age and half hidden by trailing ivy. The high Gothic windows blazed like living gold as they caught the last rays of the sun. From a beautiful turret the Penhollis flag waved gaily. The whole place breathed of tradition, of ancient Cornish ancestry, of dignity and peace.

Billie felt suddenly very small and insignificant as she looked from the great stretch of sea to Gale Towers again. She stepped out of the car and stretched cramped limbs.

'Gee!' she said, mimicking her uncle. 'It's a fine old place, Richard.'

'It's top-hole,' he said.

He spoke with fervour. He loved Cornwall: the rugged, sweeping coast; the incomparable sea. This ancient home of the Penhollis family appealed to everything in him.

Then the big oak, nail-studded door swung open. An elderly woman in a black silk gown, with cap and apron, came out to meet them. She was very dignified and very much the old type of Cornish servant.

'Welcome, sir; welcome, madam,' she said. 'We are all ready for you. Sir Percy left instructions that we were to look after you. Trenance, the butler, will see to your luggage, madam,' she added to Billie, who was about to lift her suit-case from the dicky. 'Shall I show you and the master to your room?'

Richard left Billie to answer. The girl felt her cheeks flame and her heart miss a beat. She saw at once the difficulties which would present themselves. Uncle Silas had rented Gale Towers from Sir Percy Penhollis; told him it was for the honeymoon of his niece and her husband. The servants here regarded them as a bridal pair. It was all very embarrassing, and the last thing in the world Billie wanted to deal with. But it had to be done.

'Oh, thank you,' she said as lightly as she could speak. 'Yes, do show us—er—round.'

'Thank you, madam. My name is Mrs. Massey. I'm housekeeper, and I've been with Sir Percy over twenty years or more. I was here, madam, when Sir Percy brought her ladyship back. A lovely young bride she was, too, madam—but no lovelier than yourself, if I may say so, madam!'

The ingratiating voice, the meek, downcast eyes of Mrs. Massey, and every word she spoke, irritated Billie beyond words.

'Silly old fool!' she whispered to Richard. 'I can't bear all that sort of rot. As if I do look lovely—after driving for hours—dusty, red-nosed, bad-tempered! If Mrs. Massey follows me about telling met tales of Sir Percy and his *sweet* bride (no sweeter than *I* am, mark you, Richard!), I shall go mad!'

At the moment, however, she preserved her temper, and with a grimace at her husband followed the housekeeper's portly form into the house. There a nice old butler, with white hair and mild, kindly eyes, greeted them, then went out to the car to fetch the luggage. Billie and Richard found themselves in an immense wide hall, oak panelled, and with a polished oaken floor spread with fine old Persian rugs. Antique oaken chests and chairs, walls covered with ancient relics of war, antlers' heads, hunting-horns, old fire-arms, gave the place the correct atmosphere of the baronial hall. Directly opposite the front door was a magnificent stained-glass Gothic window—a riot of vivid warm colours as the sun filtered through. At the foot of the wide staircase stood two figures on pedestals—knights in shining armour.

'Genuine armour, as worn by the Knight of King Arthur's Round Table,' the garrulous Mrs. Massey informed the newcomers as they looked about them. 'Sir Percy was descended from one of them.'

Richard caught Billie's eye. They tried to look gravely interested and not to laugh. Gale Towers was a beautiful place, full of beautiful old things, but just a little too theatrical for Billie's taste. She could quite understand why her American uncle had fallen in love with it. It was the type of old English residence, half genuine, half fake, that never fails to appeal to Americans.

Billie liked the panelling, the old war relics, and the portrait gallery of the Penhollis ancestors all the way up the staircase. They were good and interesting. But she felt she could not quite forgive the armoured knights and their visored faces!

Now came the awkward discussion upon their room. Mrs. Massey having shown them the drawing-room and dining-room—both fine, tastefully furnished and comfortable—took them upstairs to a huge bedroom on the first floor.

'Your room, madam—sir; the dressing-room for the master leads out of it. It's the room where Sir Percy and his——'

'Oh yes,' interrupted Billie hurriedly. 'I understand.'

The size of the room baffled her. It had three high windows which overlooked the sea; a perfect view of the Strand and the rolling Atlantic. The furniture was heavy, though good of its period, and a huge four-poster bed, with old-fashioned flowered-cretonne valance and curtains, made Billie's heart sink.

'Is—are there two smaller rooms?' she blurted out.

Richard hastily retired to the passage, and left his wife to deal with the housekeeper, over whose smug face a look of shocked surprise had spread. He dug his hands in his pockets and surveyed a pike in a glass case, which he supposed the venerable Sir Percy had caught in his youth.

'How I shall loathe Sir Percy before I leave this place!' he thought. 'I wonder how Billie's going to manage this question of rooms?'

Billie managed it. Quietly and firmly she convinced the astonished housekeeper that she and her husband were a modern pair—always occupied separate rooms—and must have them.

'We'll keep this—er—beautiful room with the four-poster for a guest-room,' she said. 'You can give us two single rooms, can't you, Mrs. Massey?'

'Yes, if you wish it, madam,' said Mrs. Massey in an injured voice. Obviously she was aggrieved that the 'bridal pair' should reject the bedroom in which Sir Percy and his bride had slept for so many years. She told them down in the servants' hall that she didn't know what the world was coming to.

'Separate bedrooms, indeed!—whoever heard of such a thing?—and she with her hair cropped like a boy, and a cigarette in her mouth—and talking to him so sharp-like—nobody'd think they was only married yesterday! They ought to be sharing that room of Sir Percy's and her ladyship's in a proper, decent way, I say!'

But the two single rooms were found and prepared, and the awkward moment bridged. Later down in the drawing room, Billie walked around examining china cabinets and old glass and the family miniatures and treasures, while Richard stretched his long legs in an arm-chair and smoked.

'We've shocked Mrs. Massey to the bone,' she told him. 'I

knew Uncle Silas would land us in some sort of a ditch like this!'

'Oh, well, we've got out of it,' said Richard.

He surveyed her thoughtfully. She was still in the coat and skirt and boyish silk shirt which she had worn whilst motoring. He thought she looked a trifle pale and tired.

'You've done too much motoring. You look fagged, my dear Billie,' he said, blowing a cloud of smoke toward her. 'Go to bed early to-night.'

'Oh, I'm all right. But I won't stay up late,' she said. 'Do you think if we ring for Trenance and ask for a bronx he'll stare at us in amaze?'

'We'll try,' laughed Richard.

The old butler did stare. He had never heard of a bronx. (Sir Percy did not drink cocktails.) He had gin, however, and a bottle of vermouth, which the cook used for flavouring. He was asked to bring them in. He did so and retired, convinced that the young couple were mad.

'What her ladyship would think of Mrs. Bromley, I dursen't think,' the young parlour-maid informed them down in the servants' hall. 'I've unpacked her things, and she'm got no nightgown—only pyjamas!'

Upstairs, Billie and Richard drank their gin and vermouth, and discussed the future.

'I shan't be able to stand this for long,' said Billie frankly. 'This huge place and the honeymoon atmosphere will get on my nerves.'

'Tony won't be able to come down for a week or so, and your cousin has agreed to remain with Mr. Carden till he sails next month, so what can we do?' said Richard.

Billie did not answer for a moment. She was more tired than she would admit, and her nerves had been somewhat frayed by the excitements and predicaments of the last forty-eight hours. To be married and condemned to long weeks in a solitary Cornish house was more than depressing. Already she chafed for her old freedom and independence; felt that in trying to retain her fortune she had put a heavier yoke upon herself than she had bargained for.

Richard, looking up at her through the soft shadows of twilight which were now filling the big drawing-room of Gale Towers, was amazed and dismayed to see tears in her eyes.

Billie with tears glistening on her lashes! It was so feminine and so unlike her that he was shocked. He put down his glass, rose, and went to her side.

'Why, my dear girl, what's the matter?' he exclaimed.

She dashed a slim brown hand across her eyes. She was horrified that she had allowed him to see her momentary weakness.

'Nothing's the matter,' she blurted out. 'Nothing at all.'

'Oh yes, there is. You're nearly crying.'

'How dare you? I'm not!'

'But you are. Trust me—tell me what's wrong, my dear,' he said gently.

She looked up at him. His eyes looked intensely blue in his lean, tanned face, and full of kindness. She realised suddenly what a dear he was, and how good to her. Not by word or deed since the day at Storrington when he had agreed to marry her on her own terms had he overstepped the mark, or given her a second's anxiety. She remembered Lady Jo's warning, Vera's cynicism; they had suggested that Richard would not be satisfied to live with her on platonic ground; that she would have trouble. But that was not true. He was as unwilling as she to let sentiment spoil their compact. He had said so often; he had had his lesson with his first wife.

But, at the same time, she became conscious to-night of difficulties. She dreaded the thought of long days and nights at Gale Towers, alone with Richard. Under that mask of boyishness, of hard, direct action and common sense, she was only a girl, and a very young one, and this business put a strain on her. She could not get away from the fact that she was a woman and that Richard was a man. Whatever they both felt upon matters of love, they were of opposite sex, and both were subtly, silently conscious of it.

She looked away from him, her breath quickening slightly, her face hot and red.

'Nothing's the matter. I'm only being stupid.'

'Tired, eh? You're so wilful, Billie. You try to act like a man, and drive that great car hundreds of miles without resting, and the result is you find yourself very much a girl and done in—what?'

Angry with herself for the tears that had sprung to her eyes despite all her will, and angry with him for saying what was true, she stamped one small foot.

'Not a bit. I—I may be tired, but I—I'm not done in. Nobody shall say I ever give in.'

'But, my dear girl, admit you're fagged out, and go to bed,' he said kindly. 'I can have dinner by myself. Nothing else is troubling you, is it? You can't be so frightfully upset about the exile here with me, surely!'

The unconscious male arrogance of this brought a smile to her lips.

'Oh, I don't know,' she said. 'I can't say I'm happy about it.'

'I shan't worry you or interfere with you. Don't you trust me yet?' he said, a trifle irritably.

On an impulse she put out a hand to him.

'Yes, of course. You're very decent to me, Richard. I'll give in and admit I'm tired to-night—and silly. The whole affair has knocked me off my perch a bit.'

'No wonder. I can quite imagine any woman getting the blues through being forced for mercenary motives to marry me,' he laughed dryly.

He had taken her hand and held it in a tight grasp. Under his own mask of cynicism and hardness he was immensely thrilled by her femininity revealed by her tears, and the warm softness of that slim hand which could grip the steering-wheel of her car with such skill and strength. And he was still more thrilled when she said:

'Nonsense—I'd rather be married to you, since I've had to marry—than to any other man I've known or met. You're a brick.'

'I thank you, Mrs. Bromley,' he said. He was facetious because he had the insane feeling that unless he preserved his sense of humour to-night, he would take Billie in his arms and kiss her; she looked so pale, so tired, so pathetically young for all her sharp tongue and boyish ways.

'If I kiss her, she'll immediately hate me,' he thought grimly.

By this time Billie was mistress of herself again. Awkwardly she withdrew her fingers from his.

'I'll take your advice, sir,' she said lightly, 'and hie me to my bed. You can deal with the terrible Mrs. Massey, and tell her to send up some soup or something to me.'

'Right you are,' he said. 'Good-night my child, and sleep well. In the morning we'll walk into Tintagel and go over the historic ruins and buy post cards for Tony.'

She departed, and he was left alone in the big twilit room. He felt suddenly miserable and lonely because she had gone, and he was faced with a long evening by himself.

CHAPTER 16

BILLIE went to bed and lay there resting and reading until she was ready for sleep. The weather was treacherous and the June day which had been so beautiful and sunny ended in sudden cloud, wind, and rain. One of those small summer gales that spring up so swiftly on the Cornish coast blew up from the sea that night. Billie went to sleep with the sound of the waves thundering up against the cliffs below Gale Towers, lulling her to oblivion. She loved storms. They never frightened or disturbed her. But this one disturbed Richard. He sat up half the night, smoking and staring out of the window at the dark sky, and listening to the tempestuous thunder of the waves. He could never listen to a howling wind or the sharp hiss of rain against a window-pane without thinking of Olive ... Olive who had been as frightened as a child of storms—who had seized them always as opportunities to be kissed and cuddled and petted.

Richard knew full well that the girl who was in the room adjoining this one at Gale Towers would not be afraid—was probably fast asleep. But if it had been his first wife, she would have run in to him, clung to him, blessed the delicious security of his arms.

A pain that was almost physical shook Richard's heart. He turned from the window and began to pace his room, hands in his dressing-gown pockets, face grim and set. He could not bear the rememberance of the wife who had run away from him; whose love for him had been so shallow and had lasted such a little time. It was not that he wanted her back. He never wanted to see her pretty, selfish face again. It was all that she had stood for that he wanted, because he was an ordinary, human, passionate man. If he could regain what he had lost in Olive—with Billie ... that thought was thrilling and dangerously sweet. He was beginning to realise that she was worth winning—that one word of praise from her pleased him more than countless kisses from his first wife had ever done. But his hands were tied. He could not even begin to win her, to woo her. He had made a compact and he must keep it.

The rising wind and the squall of rain that came with it seemed to get on his nerves. He suddenly sat down on his bed and ran his fingers through his dark thick hair.

'Oh, damn!' he muttered. 'Damn ... !'

It was Richard who came down to breakfast that next morning looking haggard and white. Billie had recovered her high spirits and colour, and was aggressively cheerful. She had slept soundly all through the storm. She met him in the dining-room and grinned like a mischievous boy, her hands thrust in the pockets of the green jersey which she wore with a short tweed skirt.

'Morning, Richard!' she said. 'You look washed-out. Seen

the family ghost—Sir Percy's grandfather carrying his head under his arm—eh, what?'

Richard glared at his young wife.

'No, I have not seen the family ghost,' he snapped. 'Have you?'

'Do I look like it?' she laughed. 'Not me, my friend. I am neither superstitious nor psychic—merely a normal girl with an immense aptitude for sound slumber. Don't tell me you see spooks! I must say you have the appearance of one who has kept a midnight vigil!'

'Perhaps I have,' Richard said, in the same snappy voice, then sat down and stared across the big baronial dining-room to the serving-table. Richard was hungry, and wished that the butler would appear to lift the covers from those many mysterious dishes, and produce piping hot kidney and bacon, or buttered eggs, or grilled sole. The cooking, as proved by last night's dinner, was first-rate, and Richard, being a mere male, liked his food. He certainly had no wish to spar with Billie in his present mood. He was both ashamed and worried by his emotions of last night, and wondered just what this girl would have said had he told her that he had not slept because he had been thinking about her. Not for worlds would he confess to it, though. She would either jeer at him or be annoyed.

She was looking nicer than he had seen her for many days. The long night's rest had made her complexion appear clear, with a healthy glow to the tan, and her eyes were bright and dancing. She was standing by the tall window, boyish head smooth as a chestnut and as glossy; her figure childishly slim and immature in that apple-green jersey with its black silk tie, and the rough tweed skirt only reaching to her knees. Richard turned his gaze from her and scowled heavily at the door, praying for Trenance to come and dish up the breakfast. He did not want to look at Billie. This morning she made him feel horribly old and stupid.

She was no longer interested in his pallor or the family ghost. She was looking eagerly out of the window. The sun streamed upon her. The sky was cloudless, and the sea sparkled like a great opal, blue and jade, with flashes of white where the wind caught the spray from the crest of the great rolling waves. She could just see the Gull Rock. The shrill, melancholy cries of the sea-gulls rose above the unceasing roar and splash of the incoming tide.

'Oh, Richard, it's priceless!' Billie suddenly exclaimed.

'Yes, Trebarwith and Tintagel are top-hole in the summer,' he said, in a better humour. 'We'll have a tramp round after breakfast. Come along—pour out my coffee like a dutiful wife.'

Billie grimaced and joined him at the table. The old butler was in the room now, placing grape-fruit before them. A few minutes later they were both eating busily.

Richard's brow cleared. The dangerous sentiments of last night were put away—forgotten. Once more he and Billie were good friends, bent only on getting over the difficulties and boredom of this enforced 'honeymoon.'

The morning passed pleasantly. The Vauxhall was left in the garage for a rest, and Richard and Billie set out on foot for a good long tramp along the cliffs to Tintagel. There they climbed up to the ruined castle; there from the dizzying heights surveyed that wondrous panorama of glittering sea and curved, rugged coast. Post cards were duly purchased for Tony, written, and sent off. Midday found them in the lounge of King Arthur's Castle Hotel, drinking cocktails.

'One ought to have lime-squash to be in keeping with our idyllistic surroundings,' Richard remarked as he sipped his dry Martini. 'Why don't we cut out this poison, Billie?'

She pursed her lips.

'My dear, I beg of you to refrain from making me sign the pledge as well as be the dutiful wife,' she said, with a gurgle of laughter. 'I should die of ennui if I couldn't have my cocktail.'

'You young women of to-day are a disgrace,' grumbled Richard. 'Mrs. Massey is right to be shocked. I'm sure Lady Penhollis drank a little ginger-wine or home-made sloe gin at this hour.'

'Stow it, Richard,' said Billie. 'Remember that I'm no lady, that I've been dragged up, and that I'm hideously spoiled.'

'Oh, you're not so bad,' he said, with a sudden smile.

She drained her cocktail glass hurriedly. Praise from Richard had a slightly disturbing effect, always.

'But as for being the dutiful wife, you're nothing of the kind,' he added teasingly. 'So don't flatter yourself.'

Her colour rose. She stood up and fanned her cheeks with a slim brown hand.

'I'm hot,' she said, ignoring what he said. 'Can't think why I put on such clothes in the middle of summer. I must get back and find a cotton frock.'

'And I my old flannels,' he said.

On the way back across the cliffs, their feet noiseless on the green springy turf, they were silent, lost in contemplation of the beauty of sea and sky, and the brown hilly country that lay baked and dry under the hot June sun.

Just before they reached the gates of Gale Towers, Billie turned to her companion.

'I say, Richard,' she said, 'it's all very well—we've enjoyed seeing the place this morning, and I dare say we could play a round of golf this afternoon, but we can't keep on like this alone, indefinitely.'

'I agree,' he said. 'What do you suggest?'

'We'd better hurry them up at Wimpole Street and get Tony down to relieve the monotony—or send for Vera.'

Richard frowned. Did he want Vera? He thought of her—pretty, gushing, full of soft, dainty, kittenish ways. Attractive . . . yes, to some men. Not to him. Did he want her down here in this lonely Cornish spot?

'We must do something or I shall go mad,' was Billie's next cheerful comment.

He looked at her, his eyes sardonic.

'Don't go mad,' he said. 'The most admirable quality you possess is that of sanity. We'll fix something, my dear. Uncle Silas is the snag. When does he depart for America?'

'Soon, I hope,' said Billie fervently.

They entered the great hall of the Towers, exhausted and hot after their long walk. It was deliciously cool in the big house, and especially in the hall, where the rays of the sun were tempered by the rich colours of the stained-glass window.

Trenance, the butler, met them with a telegram on a salver.

'It came half an hour ago, madam,' he said. 'For Mrs. Bromley.'

Billie opened the orange envelope with a queer little jerk of the heart. Mrs. Bromley! How queer that looked. She supposed that she would never again receive a letter or telegram addressed to Miss Carden.

She scanned the wire, then handed it to Richard.

'Oh, Gawd!' she said, shocking Trenance into a reproving look at her. 'We aren't destined to be alone long, anyhow.'

Richard read the wire. It was from Mr. Carden:

'Have to return to America sooner than expected so sure you turtle-doves will forgive old uncle for disturbing you so mighty quick after wedding. Coming down to-morrow with Vera meet afternoon train from town.—UNCLE SILAS.'

Richard handed the telegram back to his wife.

'This is a mixed blessing,' he said. 'Do we or do we not want Uncle Silas and Cousin Vera?'

'It might relieve the monotony,' said Billie. 'On the other hand, Uncle Silas is sure to be trying, and we shall be made to twine on the sofa or I shall be asked to tinkle on Lady Penhollis's spinnet while you lean both arms upon it and gaze into my soulful eyes. I can see all sorts of horrors presenting themselves!'

Richard could not help smiling.

'Little devil,' he said under his breath.

Her grey-green eyes sparkled at him.

'Well, isn't it true? You can see from that wire what Uncle Silas thinks us. *Turtle-doves* ...!'

She collapsed into a chair in the drawing-room and closed her eyes.

'I'm exhausted, Richard. Order me a long drink—lemon-squash, this time, or both Trenance and Mrs. Massey will think me the worst woman in Cornwall!'

When they had finished laughing over the telegram, they lapsed into more gloomy reflections. Mr. Carden had made things difficult in London on the wedding-day. His arrival with Vera might break the monotony, but assuredly it would mean a fresh strain. The more Billie considered the situation, the more worried she became. But Richard viewed it with altogether novel sensations. He was just a little excited. It would be amusing to 'play up' for Uncle Silas's benefit; interesting to make pretence of being a lover-like husband to Billie.

His own thoughts baffled and perplexed him.

'Seems to me I'm changing rapidly,' he thought. 'Down in Sussex, before Billie came into my life, I was cynical, sick of women, a confirmed bachelor. Now I'm becoming my old self—the Richard who made such a fool of himself over Olive!'

It would never do, he mentally argued. It would lead to disaster. Far better to remain hard and passionless. The girl whom he had married would hate and resent any sign of weakness from him. He would lose her friendship and her trust if he allowed sentiment to master him. Yet one alarming fact was beginning to present itself clearly. His feelings for Billie were undergoing transformation—subtle but sure. He could not regard her as a boy, as a 'pal,' a partner in a mercenary business transaction. She was a woman and an attractive one at that, and her very coolness, aloofness, were beginning to challenge the warm, passionate man in him—the lover he was at heart.

Billie left him to tell Mrs. Massey about the visitors coming to-morrow. He slowly filled his pipe and stuck it in his mouth. His teeth clenched a little over the briar stem.

'Fool!' he said to himself. 'Idiot, Richard Bromley. You'll

103

make a mess of things if you aren't careful!'

He was thankful that Billie suggested golf for the afternoon. Under the circumstances he did not wish to laze about the place doing nothing. His thoughts turned too often to Billie and that slender wedding-ring which he had placed upon her finger two days ago.

They were both tired out after the day's exercise when evening came, and both glad to go to bed before ten o'clock. And this time Richard slept like a log the night through, undisturbed until Trenance took him his early tea.

The post that morning brought a letter from Tony to his elder brother. He had taken his first walk yesterday—was 'frightfully bucked about it,' and hoped to join them in Cornwall next week.

'Dear old Tony,' Richard said to his wife at breakfast-time. 'It's amazing to me to think he can walk again. We owe that to you, Billie, and——'

'Poof!' she broke in, 'not to me at all—to the man who operated on him. I'm jolly glad the kid can walk. It will be a pleasure to see him down here.'

He looked at her with pure affection in his eyes. He liked her in that cool striped-silk tennis frock. It made her much more feminine. And suddenly, uncontrolled, he said:

'You're rather a darling, Billie!' Then he turned from her, flushing up to the roots of his hair. She stared at his back, amazed. To cover his confusion, he began to talk about trains from Camelford, and what time they were to meet Uncle Silas and Vera. He gave her no chance to reproach him for the endearment, and even had he done so, she was not quite certain what she would have said. She was shocked into speechlessness. She had never been called 'a darling' by a man before. People did not address her in such terms. '*A darling!*' Billie felt almost indignant. One applied that word to silly, fluffy women or children. What was Richard thinking of? It was not a thing she would have expected him to say.

She made no comment upon it, and in a few minutes' time

was deep in a discussion about Tony's journey to Cornwall. But she did not forget that unexpected outburst from Richard. It disturbed her strangely for the rest of the day.

Richard was shocked at himself and terrified that he had annoyed her; but since she ignored it, he gradually became easy in his mind, and told himself that he had better be careful not to give way to his feelings again.

CHAPTER 17

THEN Uncle Silas and Vera arrived.

Mr. Carden was bursting with enthusiasm to see the 'young pair' in their furnished house, which he insisted upon calling 'Honeymoon Hall.' He declared they both looked browner and happier than ever, raved about the Cornish coast and the Penhollis possession, and was generally content. Vera was quieter, but just as eager to see Billie and her husband 'at home.' Inwardly, she was burning with curiosity. She thought Richard most attractive and more handsome than she remembered him, in his white flannels, strolling about Gale Towers, looking like a sunburned boy instead of a man well over thirty. But she fancied she saw a new look in his very blue eyes—when he rested his gaze upon his wife.

Vera was a fool about most things, but clever as regards the ways of a man with a maid. She was certain, before she had been down to Gale Towers twenty-four hours, that Richard had fallen in love with his wife—or at least was toppling, if he had not already fallen. Billie seemed to her just the same—blunt, boyish, unconcerned.

'What a mug she is!' was Vera's inward comment. 'I'd give the world to have Richard Bromley at *my* feet!'

She was at her very best now that she had arrived; not too pushing with Richard—just affectionately sweet and modest and appealing. To Billie she was charming, only just showing a fraction of that claw under the velvet glove.

'You must be divinely happy, Billie dear,' she murmured when she was alone with her cousin in the latter's bedroom, for the first time that day, while Billie dressed for dinner.

'Vera, I shall push you over the cliff if you start that rot,' said Billie shortly. 'I'm bored to sobs, and you know it.'

'But it's such a lovely house, darling, and Richard is so nice to you. What woman could want a more adorable husband?'

'The words "darling" and "adorable" don't exist in my vocabulary,' said Billie, lighting a cigarette. 'Richard is very nice and a very good friend.'

Vera cast her lashes downward and reflected. She thought she could see how the land lay. Billie was unaltered. But Richard Bromley was just what she had prognosticated—an ordinary male— and he was *not* going to be content with friendship.

'The fun begins,' mused Vera.

'You don't regret your marriage—yet, then?' was Vera's next remark.

'Not a bit,' said Billie calmly. 'Uncle Silas is content, and I've kept my money, and Tony can walk, so we're all satisfied.'

'I'm glad,' said Vera in her sweetest voice.

'I can hear Uncle Silas singing "Pasadena" in his bath,' said Billie, picking up a brush and vigorously attacking her shingled head. 'Richard will be down by this time. He's always dressed first. You're ready, V., so you go down and amuse him.'

Vera was only too ready to comply with this request. She hastened down to the hall. Trenance, passing through, informed her that Mr. Bromley was in the library. This room—big, cool, with olive-green carpet and walls lined with handsomely bound books—was still full of the late summer sunshine. It annoyed Vera. She disliked herself in evening-dress in broad daylight. She was conscious, however, of looking quite pretty in her pale pink georgette frock, flat-pleated and simple in design. She seemed very youthful and dainty, with her golden head, wide blue eyes, and pastel-pink cheeks. Those cheeks were a natural carmine just now as she entered the library and greeted Richard, who was deep in a book by an open window. Her foolish heart beat fast when he stood up and looked at her. Surely he would admire her. Men did, as a rule. She was made to be petted and spoiled, and to stir up all the most dangerous and ignoble feelings in the stronger sex.

'Hullo!' she murmured. 'Isn't it a lovely night? And what a fascinating house. I'm sure it's haunted.'

'Billie was talking of family ghosts the other evening,' smiled Richard. 'Sit down—there's a comfortable chair.'

He drew up one of the deep, leather-cushioned armchairs, and she sank into it. Against the dark olive she looked like a delicately coloured flower in her pale pink gown. She leaned her golden head back, quite conscious of the picture she made.

'What a chair!' she laughed. 'It swallows me up.'

He offered her a cigarette, lit it for her, then sat back in his own chair, discussing haunted houses. But he was bound to notice that Billie's cousin was very pretty indeed, and as unlike that sun-browned, abrupt young woman as she could be.

'A magazine-cover girl,' he reflected, while he talked to her. 'Useless—just like those white little hands! Olive had hands like that.'

Strange, how Vera put him in mind of his first wife! She was looking up at him with big, soft eyes, just as Olive used to do. It irritated rather than attracted him.

'How d'you think Billie looks?' he asked abruptly.

'Just the same as ever. And how do you like your strange marriage, Cousin Richard?'

He wished she would not call him 'Cousin Richard.' He

was not her cousin, and it was merely a pose. But she posed all the time. He realised that. He smiled a little dryly.

'I'm quite happy, thank you—Cousin Vera.'

'How extraordinary!' Vera sighed.

'Why?'

She drooped her long fair lashes and flicked her cigarette ash into the bronze tray on the little Queen Anne table beside her. 'Oh—I don't know,' she said evasively.

'Why shouldn't I be happy?' he asked in a tone of defiance that proved to her cunning little mind that he was not.

'Well, I shouldn't be,' she said slowly. 'But then I have such different theories about marriage.'

'You mean you are one of the many misguided ones who believe in love, eh?'

'Yes, I do,' she said, raising her head and giving him the full benefit of her eyes now—beautiful, guileless blue eyes that would mislead most men. He shrugged his shoulders and smiled at her in the same dry fashion.

'I take it you don't approve of our cut-and-dried affair then?' he said.

'It's not my business, of course,' she said, with her sweet smile. 'But I just couldn't do it if I were Billie. I'd rather lose my money than marry without love.'

'I wonder,' mused Richard. 'I'm not so sure!'

'But of course,' added Vera, 'you don't believe in love, like Billie, and I suppose you don't feel the lack of it.'

That shaft went home, as it was meant to do. He stiffened and looked unsmilingly out of the window at the sunset. Vera's apparently artless remark brought back the dangerous reflections of two nights ago—the thoughts he had been doing his level best to eradicate from his brain. He had begun to feel the lack of love—of a woman's tenderness and attention—and he knew it. His intimate companionship with Billie, his strange marriage to her, and their isolation down here, had all worked on emotions which he had imagined dead—which he had meant to annihilate after Olive had left him. He wished heartily that Vera would let well alone, and not attempt to discuss his feelings. Deliberately he broached a new subject.

'How is Uncle Silas?' he said curtly.

Vera was disappointed. She would like to have continued the discussion about Billie's marriage. She felt that Richard had given her a silent rebuff. With a good grace, however, she answered his polite inquiry about Mr. Carden. But his very disinclination to talk about love and matrimony was fresh proof that he was not altogether the cold, platonic friend of Billie's imagination. And one of these days he would grow tired of Billie's friendship, and want more ... then little doubt he would be rejected ... and would turn to another woman on the rebound.

Vera fully intended to be that woman when the time came.

Her *tête-à-tête* with Richard was brought to an end by Uncle Silas and Billie, who came down together. Vera, watching like a tigress watches its prey, saw Richard's gaze flash past Mr. Carden to his wife. It was a look of intense interest, if nothing more. And Billie was unconscious of it. She was very quietly dressed to-night in her black lace gown, which was sleeveless and cool. She wore her pearls to please her uncle, and the ring which had belonged to Richard's mother.

It pleased Richard to see her wear that ring. He did not intend to lose control of himself again. Uncle Silas was here. It was necessary to act a part, but to go warily to-night.

Uncle Silas rubbed his hands together, and surveyed his niece and nephew-in-law with twinkling little eyes.

'Well, you two—say, it's a treat to be down here in this lovely western air, after London. Ain't you enjoying it?'

'Very much,' said Billie.

'Rather,' seconded Richard.

'I've been having a talk with Mrs. Massey,' said Mr. Carden, with a sly look at Richard. 'Quaint old bird, isn't she? Some knowledge of the Penhollis history. She's real put out because you two wouldn't have that room with the four-poster. Told me all her grievances!'

Billie's cheeks burned. Richard cleared his throat.

'Never mind,' continued the terrible old man, 'No need for blushes. I told the good Mrs. Massey that times have changed, and young folk to-day like separate rooms. It don't make any difference to the lovin'. Not that I've seen you kiss your little gurl once to-day, Richard, my boy. Go and give her a real good one right now. Ain't she lookin' sweet to-night?'

Richard did not move. But his eyes met those of his wife. She said silently, 'Isn't he *awful?*'

'I'm not—er—very keen on public embraces, Uncle Silas,' he blurted out, for her sake.

'Tush, tush,' said Mr. Carden, laughing. 'Vera and I ain't public. Don't be shy. I reckon you Englishmen are stiff as pokers. Go on, boy—let's see you be a real Rudolph Valentino!'

He gave them no chance to refuse or wriggle out of it. Billie, with red-hot cheeks and a clenched fist, would like to have told Uncle Silas that he was an irritating old idiot. But she dared not. He laboured under the delusion that she had married for love, and after all, what real married lovers would refuse to kiss, or be angry about it?

Richard advanced toward her. She muttered the words she had used before, that day at the Ritz:

'Come on—get it over . . .!'

'Not on the cheek like that last peck you gave her,' said Mr. Carden, with his rollicking laugh. 'A real kiss, my boy!'

'Oh, damn!' said Richard, *sotto voce*. And he swore not because he did not want to kiss Billie, but because he *did* . . .

Vera, from her arm-chair, hung forward, lips parted, eyes bright with excitement. She was enjoying this little drama. She wanted to see just what Richard would do—and just how Billie would take the enforced caress. But Uncle Silas, quite unaware of the conflicting feelings of the 'young people,' looked on with amusement, his short, stout body quivering with mirth. He was recollecting that honeymoon in Pasadena with his Sally . . . gee! what fun it had been to snatch a kiss or two from that sweetheart whom he had married 'way down south!

'Say, go ahead, Richard!' he urged. 'Why, bo', you're the shyest I've struck in Old England yet. Give her a real bind-it-down one. She'll like it!'

Richard was close to his wife now. He was surprised to see how white she was. Her slender figure was trembling with suppressed rage.

'Vulgar old brute!' she said through her teeth. 'Oh, I wish I'd given up the money—anything rather than go through this!'

She supposed Richard was equally angry. How could she guess that he was shaking—not with rage, but with the passion he was trying to control. He, too, was white. But his eyes smiled, looked darkly blue under their thick dark brows. And suddenly his arms went round her, drew her up against him.

'Sorry, my dear,' he whispered, with a short laugh. 'But it's got to be done . . .'

Billie, in that strong embrace, had the paralysing sensation of a trapped creature, unable to escape. She also had the insane desire to scream and push him away with her clenched fists. But the next instant he had bent his head and his lips were on her mouth. It was a very brief kiss. Within a second she was free again, and he was walking away from her, and Uncle Silas was rocking with laughter. But Billie did not laugh. She stood stock still, her face as hotly crimson as it had been white, her hands doubled at her sides. The effect of that kiss was indescribable. For although fleeting, it had not been a light, friendly salute. It had had passion in it . . .and passion had never touched Billie before . . . never in her life.

Instinctively she recalled her dream of days ago, before her marriage with Richard—the dream in which she had been caught to his heart and passionately kissed. She gave a little gasp and swung round, walked to the open window. She wanted fresh air—leaned her head right out so that the cool evening breeze coming up from the sea could fan her burning face. In that moment she hated Richard—felt humiliated by that kiss. How dared he? ... it was not playing the game ... he could have pretended ... but that kiss ... his lips had been hard, hot against her mouth.

Richard, who had plunged into conversation with Mr. Carden, looked at Billie, whose back was turned to him now. His heart pounded like a sledge-hammer, although he talked lightly and easily to the old man who was the cause of all the trouble. He was fully aware that he had overstepped the mark—possibly offended Billie beyond forgiveness. He knew that the kiss he had laid upon her mouth had been no pretence—knew now how desperately he had wanted to kiss her. Yet he could not be sorry, could not feel ashamed. Even though he had broken his compact with her, he had been true to himself at last—given way to the natural human impulses which he had scorned since Olive had run away from him. And whatever happened now, he realised one thing—one great fact which was unspeakably sweet and thrilling. He loved Billie ... *loved her*. Out of that sole embrace to-night had sprung an enduring passion.

His breath quickened as he continued to stare at that slender, black-clad figure by the open window.

'You hate me now,' he thought. 'You won't trust me any more, perhaps. But I don't care. If I never kiss you again on earth, I love you ... you dear ... you darling!'

And this was the old Richard ... the ardent lover ... the warm, impulsive man who would go a thousand miles to be with the woman he loved for one half-hour.

'I'm mad, mad,' he told himself. 'I was happier down in Storrington with Tony, hating women, jeering at love. But I was too confident of my strength ... I ought never to have married Billie under such conditions—never!'

But it was too late for self-reproach or regret. The thing had been done. Billie was his wife. And he had fallen in love with her. It had its humorous side, he reflected grimly. And it was not the kind of love that he had given Olive. For her he had felt the tender, protective affection which a man feels for a soft, helpless, fluffy woman ... the hot, headstrong passion of a boy for his first love, his wife. His feeling for Billie was different and much more lasting. For there was comradeship behind it. He had liked and respected her as he would have done a clean-minded fearless boy. He could no longer look upon her as Billie, the boy. She was a girl ... and to-night he had felt all the sweetness, the womanly softness of that slim body in his arms ... had thrilled in every fibre of his being when he had laid that brief, passionate kiss on her mouth.

One thing, however, was certain. He must not let her know that he cared *this* way ... must somehow make her forget that kiss. Otherwise he would lose her altogether. The mere idea now of losing Billie, of living without her, dismayed him.

'Pull up—pull up, you fool!' he mentally raged at himself. 'You're going all to pieces ...'

Billie turned from the window. She had recovered. She was smiling now. But when Richard's blue eyes met hers in an agony of anxiety, she ignored the appeal in them; looked straight through, then past him.

He knew, then, how deeply he had offended her.

CHAPTER 18

WITH a heart like lead he went in to dinner. But even though he was worried, furious with himself for his lack of control, he exulted deep down within him ... the natural exultation of the man who has found the One and Only Woman in the world.

The exultant feeling was crushed, however, before the end of the evening. Billie studiously avoided him, refused to either look at or speak to him more than was necessary for her uncle's benefit.

Silas G. Carden was much too occupied in examining the Penhollis plate and silver, and cabinets of treasures, to notice anything amiss. But Vera saw the thunder-cloud on her cousin's brow, and was aware of Richard's gloom. And she guessed exactly what had happened.

'It will all work out just as I have prophesied,' she reflected, with amusement. 'These two are working up for a row!'

She set herself out to be charming to Richard that evening. He talked to her politely and applauded when she sat down at the piano and sang one or two light love-songs in a pretty soprano. But his thoughts were far, far away from Vera. He could scarcely take his eyes off his young wife. He felt depressed and remorseful because she would not meet his eye.

'I've said all the way along that love is a rotten business and only leads to disaster,' he told himself ironically. 'Now I've let myself in for it again, thrice-cursed fool that I am!'

He felt he could not continue like this with Billie, that whatever happened he must regain her favour, her friendship, and quell that tumult of longing which the very sight and sound of her was arousing in him.

He was thankful when Uncle Silas retired, assuring them he had enjoyed himself heartily, and Vera (bored and yawning) followed him. He was left alone with his wife. She moved toward the door, her brown head very erect, obviously intending to leave him and go to bed. But Richard put out a hand and detained her.

'Oh—er—just a minute, Billie,' he said awkwardly. 'I—er—want a word with you.'

She turned round. Her eyes were hard—just like grey-green stones seen through clear water.

'What do you want?' she asked coldly.

'Come and have a cigarette, Billie,' he said. 'We haven't said half a word to each other to-night.'

Billie felt indignant. It was colossal impudence on his part to talk to her as though nothing had happened. She tilted her head higher.

'No thanks,' she said shortly. 'I want to go to bed.'

'But I want to talk to you,' he insisted.

'What about?'

'Oh, my dear old thing,' he said, with a nervous laugh. 'Have we quarrelled, or are we about to quarrel? What is it?'

Behind her mask of coldness and composure, Billie's temper was raging. She had a hot temper when it was roused. And suddenly it broke through and poured over him.

'You're a cad—a perfect beast!' she said, her cheeks flaming, her hands trembling, clenched at her sides. 'You know exactly what the quarrel is. How dared you kiss me like that? How *dared* you?'

Richard swore softly under his breath. He was 'in for it' now, and no mistake, he reflected. He would have given much to have gathered this proud, angry little figure up into his arms and kissed her until she was breathless. But he did not dare. He was fully aware that he must play his cards tactfully and with skill, unless he wished to lose her for ever. But oh, how he loved her—how he admired her—how he wanted her, this slim concentrated fury with hard lips and eyes! What a heaven lay in store for the man who could win her; turn her into soft, yielding woman in his arms!

He controlled himself perfectly, however. He realised that he had angered her and made her mistrustful, and he was genuinely eager to regain her faith and friendship. He *was* a cad—she was right, he thought. He had had no right to kiss her like that after the promises he had made, and considering the compact upon which he had agreed. He ought to have kept an iron hand on his emotions. The kiss had been fatal to himself. He would love her, go on loving her now till the end of all things. But he kept those sentiments well under in this moment. He determined to lie shamelessly, to act a part, to do anything to put her once more at her ease. Poor little girl! She was not only annoyed, but possibly frightened of what next he might do. Why had he not realised that before? He had frightened her ... made her bitterly regret her marriage and her belief in him. It would never do.

Richard was a good actor. He stared at her with every evidence of amazement. Then he pulled his cigarette-case from his pocket and handed it to her.

'My dear child, what a tornado!' he drawled. 'Have a cigarette and calm down, then tell me what I've done.'

His cool, unconcerned manner and voice had the desired effect. Billie calmed down, took the cigarette, lit it, then smoked furiously, marched across the room, and sat down on the arm of a chair. Her colour died away, but her hands were still shaking.

'I think you know quite well what you've done,' she said, at length. 'You took advantage of me—of—of my disgusting old uncle's passion to see us "spoon" as he vulgarly calls it, and you—you——'

'Well—what?' he broke in calmly. He, also, sat on the arm of a chair opposite her, smoking, watching her.

Her angry eyes met his, then drooped. A pang of compunction smote him as he looked at the brown bent head. Poor, dear little girl—she was being made to feel thoroughly nervous and uncomfortable. She was right. He was a cad. But he had to go on with this—to act the part right through. If he let her know that he realised just how he had transgressed, and confessed it was because he cared, all would be over between them. She would probably walk right out of Gale Towers to-morrow, with or without Uncle Silas G. Carden's money. The best—the only thing for him to do was to pretend ignorance and laugh at her—make her wretched because she had made a mistake—but put her at her ease with him.

'You know,' she broke out. 'You know that there was no need to—to kiss me like that, and I—oh, I *hated* it!'

It was his turn to look away from her. He had not hated that kiss. He had adored it—just as he adored her. But he shrugged his shoulders and expressed great surprise.

'My dear Billie, don't be so stupid. Of course I had to kiss you. Your uncle gave me no loophole of escape, and he stipulated that it must be on the lips. It's all so childish——'

'Oh no—it's no use saying that!' she interrupted, her head flung back again, her eyes blazing at him. 'You went too far, Richard—you—you could have hoodwinked Uncle Silas—just pretended to kiss me. I consider you didn't play fair. I said when I made the compact between us that all rot of that sort was to be cut out.'

His heart sank. Little hope, he thought grimly, of ever wooing or winning this girl. She seemed as hard as nails. But he went on with the game he had set himself out to play.

'Oh, come, my dear!' he protested. 'You're making a mountain out of a molehill. I had to kiss you. You don't think I wanted to, do you?'

That brought the scarlet to her cheeks. He prayed mentally for forgiveness for that shameless lie.

'I didn't want to kiss you,' he went on. 'I was fed up with the whole affair. I just acted nicely to please your wretched uncle, and this is my reward—you take it seriously!'

Billie stared at him. For the first time she wavered, wondering whether she had been a little idiot and accused him wrongfully.

'I'm amazed at you, Billie,' he continued. 'How *could* you think I was breaking the compact? I regret that I had to kiss you, and I shall certainly never do it again. Uncle Silas will be returning to New York soon, then there'll be no need to act a part. If he tries on any stuff like that again, I shall lose my temper and kiss Vera.'

That was very skilful. It mollified Billie. Her lips trembled into a smile. She flung her cigarette into the grate. Of course if he had been just acting, how could she be furious or lose faith in him? She was ridiculous. She had been terrified of that man who had held her so close and kissed her with such passion. But this cool, careless, cynical Richard was the one she knew and liked and trusted. On an impulse she thrust out a hand.

'Sorry, old thing,' she said curtly. 'I've been an idiot. Only I hated being kissed. Don't ever do it again—you act much too well for my liking. Now let's forget it.'

He took the hand with assumed lightness, pressed it, then dropped it again. He knew he was forgiven and that his lies had put her at her ease.

'Right-o, Billie,' he said. 'I agree with you—it was a bit steep, but it won't happen again. You and I weren't cut out for that love-stuff.'

She was smiling at him now.

'You're right, Richard. As you say, you shall kiss Vera next time Uncle Silas is so insistent.'

'I've no wish to kiss anybody,' he lied.

Then he turned his face from her. He was too sick at heart to say any more, to carry on the farce any further to-night.

It was the end, of course ... the end to any hope of taking this girl in his arms again. She was his wife, but not for him. Henceforward he must be strictly, rigidly controlled—never let her dream that he cared, that he wanted her. He had regained her friendship. Now it was up to him to keep it.

He was wrapped in profound gloom when he sought his own room that night. For he knew that life with Billie was no longer going to be an amusing, easy thing of camaraderie. He loved her—hungered for her. How was he going to bear living under the same roof with her for an indefinite number of years—just as a friend?

Billie went to bed quite undisturbed by any such difficult feelings as harassed poor Richard. Indeed, she felt quite light-hearted, and hummed a tune under her breath as she slid into her tussore pyjamas, then like a slim boy, with feet apart, stood before her mirror, vigorously brushing her head with two brushes.

She was much relieved by what Richard had said. Earlier in the evening—after that terrifying embrace—she had been depressed by the suspicion that Richard was 'a cad' and not to be trusted. She had pictured dreadful, difficult scenes impending; perhaps a big row, then herself marching away for good, whether Uncle Silas disinherited her or not. But now she felt at ease and gay once more. It was she who had made a mistake and been stupidly sensitive. Richard had been acting. He did not want to kiss her. He had stated, definitely, that he did not—that he would as soon kiss Vera.

Billie grinned at her sun-browned face reflected in the mirror, set down her brushes, then lit a cigarette and smoked reflectively, perched on the end of the bed. The old impish light danced in her eyes.

'What a sell for me!' she thought. 'Richard had me cold tonight. A nice idiot I made of myself, raging at him for nothing! He's a dear—a thorough good sort; I might have known he wouldn't let me down!'

She could laugh at Lady Jo, or at Vera, who had warned her that this marriage would end in disaster. They did not know Richard Bromley as she knew him!

She finished her cigarette, and was about to slip into bed when a tap came on the door.

'*Entrez!*' said Billie, in her best French.

In walked Vera, with a pale blue silken wrapper, edged with white swansdown, over one of those transparent apologies for a nightgown that Billie despised. She looked extremely pretty, however, and Billie gave her a tolerant smile.

'Well, my handsome, what do you want?' she said, sitting with her knees tucked up under her chin.

Vera sat down gracefully on the bed.

'Oh, I've just come for a chat, Billie. What are you grinning for? Anybody'd think you were enjoying life.'

'So I am—immensely,' said Billie. 'Aren't you?'

'Oh yes—I've had quite a lot of fun going about with Uncle Silas, but I don't think I'm going to enjoy life down here.'

'Why not? No young men about, I suppose! Why, poor old Vera, it's a shame!' teased Billie. 'There's only Richard.'

'Who has no eyes for anybody but you,' said Vera. She was convinced that remarks of that sort would keep Billie permanently up in arms against Richard, which was exactly what she, Vera, wanted.

She was surprised to find that Billie did not take the

observation in good fun. The impish grin was replaced by a look of severity and annoyance.

'I object to that sort of remark, Vera,' she said sharply. 'It's stupid and untrue.'

'Neither,' said Vera, shrugging her shoulders. 'I'm quite certain your precious man of stone is flesh and blood, and rapidly thawing to you, my dear.'

'Nothing of the kind.'

'Come, Bill, I'm no fool, and I saw him kiss you to-night.'

'For Uncle Silas's benefit, entirely.'

'Then he's a first-rate actor. He looked as though he were in paradise.'

Billie sprang off the bed and faced her cousin with cheeks crimson, lips set.

'You're wrong—absolutely wrong, Vera,' she flashed. 'I tell you Richard was acting for Uncle Silas. He didn't want to kiss me any more than I wanted to be kissed.'

Vera bit her lower lip.

'Oh, all right, Billie; don't lose your temper,' she said. 'Only I thought you were fairly upset with him for the rest of the evening.'

This truth made Billie's cheeks a deeper scarlet.

'Oh, go to bed and stop thinking about it at all—it's not your affair,' she snapped. 'And for goodness' sake, V., if you want to be friends with me, keep off this love and emotion rot. You know that I hate it. And set your mind at rest about Richard. He and I are good pals, and nothing more. I'm tired now, my dear, so run along.'

Vera accepted her dismissal quite smilingly. She was used to what she called 'Billie's rudeness,' and never argued with her for long. There was too much money behind it—too much to be lost by a serious quarrel. But there were times when Vera yearned to be venomous and thoroughly rude in return.

'Right-o, Bill—night-night,' she murmured. 'Sorry I've annoyed you. I expect it's only my stupid, sentimental imagination.'

'Quite so,' said Billie dryly. 'Night, old thing.'

Vera retired and closed the bedroom door behind her. In the corridor, on her way to her own room, she ran straight into Richard, who was coming from the bath. She stepped back, a pretty picture of confusion, cheeks carnation pink, blue eyes modestly lowered.

'Oh, I'm so sorry, Cousin Richard.'

He, much more genuinely confused, because he was in a striped pyjama suit, towel round his neck, and no dressing-gown, muttered an apology, and would have fled, but she detained him.

'You're just the person I want,' she said, with a tinkling laugh. 'Have you a match with you? I've got some cigarettes but no light.'

Richard dived into a pocket and produced a box of matches.

'Here you are,' he said.

It was necessary to look at her then, and to see what a charming picture she made, with ruffled golden hair and the dainty blue wrapper, just hinting at rounded curves. She saw the look, and was content.

'Good-night,' she murmured. 'Sleep well.'

'Goodnight,' he said, and hastened off to his own room. Once there he walked to the open window and stared moodily out at a sky that blazed with stars.

'Why didn't I meet Billie instead of Vera?' he thought. 'I'd like to have seen her for a second—said good-night again.'

Poor Richard! He was in love—in love once more—and this time very badly—for it was with a wife who never would be other than wife in name. He thrust his fingers through his thick dark hair, found it wet and rough after his bath. Mechanically he began to dry it with the towel.

'Oh damn!' he muttered. 'Damn everything! That blue-eyed pet with her "Cousin Richard," and every word a caress, isn't what I want! I want Billie. But if I don't try and cut it out, I shall lose my head again and make a hideous mess of everything!'

He could not sleep. He was too harassed. He crept down to the library long after the rest of the house was wrapped in slumber, and wrote a long letter to his young brother, telling him to come down to Cornwall at the first possible moment. Tony would want looking after. That would give him something to do—something apart from Billie.

CHAPTER 19

ONE week later Uncle Silas left Gale Towers, and returned to America. He departed in the best of spirits, convinced that Billie was married to the right man, and that he could rest assured that when he died his money would go to a happily married woman and the nicest Englishman for a husband she could have found.

'I'm real pleased with you, kid,' he told Billie when he bade her farewell. 'Now I can get back to lil ole Noo York and make my will in peace. You were a sensible girl to do what I asked and to marry a bo' like Dick Bromley.'

Billie was naturally most relieved by her uncle's departure. She had found him very trying, and she was quite sure Richard had found him equally so. Now they need no longer act or pretend. There was nobody to bother about—except Tony. And Tony did not make requests for public embraces between his brother and sister-in-law. In his quiet, sentimental way he took it for granted that Richard and Billie were happy and in love, and knew that Richard was not the type of man to show emotion before others. He could see for himself that the young couple were the best of friends, and that was all that mattered.

Tony came down to Gale Towers on the day Mr. Carden departed. At the end of a fortnight he was a different being, walking by the aid of a stick, sun-browned, blissfully happy. They could scarcely recognise him as the white, miserable, pain-racked Tony who had gone into the nursing-home.

The boy was passionately grateful to Billie. He realised that he owed his marvellous recovery to her. Her money—her introduction to the big Harley Street surgeon—her doing—all of it! The delight of being up and about on his feet after the years of spinal trouble was limitless, and his devotion to Billie, his gratitude for what she had done, also unlimited.

To Richard it was pure pleasure to see his young brother walking about, taking fervent interest in life again. He, too, was deeply grateful to Billie. But he knew her too well to express that gratitude.

It was now the middle of July. Richard and Billie had been married for a month, and except for that one perilous moment on the night Mr. Carden had come down to Cornwall, they had had no difference of opinion. They were good friends. Richard had set an iron heel on his emotions. Not by word or look did he convey the hunger, the love he felt for his wife.

They were quite a happy party—for a little while—Richard, Billie, Vera and the convalescent Tony. They went for picnics on the beach, bathed twice a day, gloried in the heat which was tempered for them down on that radiant Cornish coast by cool sea-breezes and the sparkling blue water that was so invigorating and crystal clear.

With every passing day Billie proved herself an excellent companion to Richard. She was a strong swimmer—raced him through the breakers far out from shore until he grew tired and laughingly pleaded for respite. They left Vera, who was a surf-bather, with Tony, who could only paddle and look on.

Richard loved these days—gloried in the strength, the fearlessness, the splendour of his wife's womanhood. He loved to see her, beautiful brown, drenched with spray, swimming at his side in her tight black silken suit. No frilly costume or pretty cap for Billie. She left the frivolous attire to Vera. She was ever the boy, careless that her shingled head was immersed in the water; that her arms and legs were naked to the hot summer sun, burned to dark golden tan. She liked to swim back to shore and sit on a rock; drying in the sunlight, rub her wet head with a towel, a cigarette between her lips. Richard would lie on the sand at her feet, shade his eyes with his hands and stare at her, trying to resign himself to the fact that this was how things would always be between them. They would go on being just friends—nothing more.

He was her slave now—desperately, wholly in love with her. He wanted to throw himself before her, let her put one of those brown feet upon him; glory in his submission, in her mastership. His mind ached with the thought of her, with vain dreams of what life might have been had she cared for him. Would she always be boyish, hard, deaf and dumb and blind to the call of the real woman in her? Would she ever love any man, let alone the one she had married?

The answer to all these questions seemed 'no.' She was changeless, unchanging. And he dared not let her guess the torment of his feelings lest she might go from him for ever. He lived now in perpetual fear that he might lose her. She had told him that, once her uncle went back to America, she would go on with the old independent life—live apart from him. How long, then, would she stay down here in Cornwall; how long would she give him her companionship?

Billie, for the moment, had no thought of leaving Cornwall. She adored open-air life, and found Trebarwith Strand an incomparable place wherein to spend the hot summer months. Richard never failed her—he was always ready to do anything she wanted, and in the way she wanted, and if he was less grim, less cynical than the Richard she had married, she did not notice it. He treated her 'like a pal,' and that was all she had asked. In her queer blunt way she was beginning to be fond of him and to rely on his friendship. No—she had no wish to pack up and disappear—yet.

But Vera was watching and waiting. She knew Billie so well; knew the sudden, mad impulses to which the spoiled young heiress was given. One of these days she would grow sick of rustic life in Cornwall. She would want to rush off to France or Spain; take the car and do a solitary tour without Richard, without anybody. She was not going to be bound down just because she wore a wedding-ring on her finger. Frequently she had said so.

Then what would Richard have to say? What would he do? At any rate, Vera believed her hour would come. She was good at waiting for what she wanted. And with something of real passion in her foolish, shallow little heart, she wanted this man whom Billie had married.

One afternoon toward the end of July, Richard and Billie were going back to Gale Towers along the sands from Trebarwith, where they had been bathing. The tide was right out, and the sands virgin gold under the sun. Richard was comparatively happy. He loved his moments alone with his wife. Tony was tired after a morning on the beach, and had stayed at home. Vera was also resting. But Billie was tireless, full of splendid vitality. She was walking briskly along the sun-warmed beach at his side, swinging her swimming suit and towel in one hand, the inevitable cigarette in the other.

Suddenly she turned a brown, laughing face to her companion.

'Race you over those rocks,' she said, pointing to some flat rocks ahead, which were covered with wet, shining seaweed.

'Too slippery,' he said.

'Rot—funk!' she jeered.

'Oh, am I?' said Richard. 'Go on, then!'

She began to run, panting, breathless, eyes like stars. He raced after her, got ahead of her, fleet though she was. The next moment he had sprung on to the first rock, slithered over the dangerous, gleaming strips of seaweed, floundered a second, with arms thrown outwards, then crashed full length on to the dripping slab and rolled off on to the sand.

Billie reached him. All the colour left her face as she saw him lying there, absolutely still and silent.

'Richard!' she exclaimed. 'I say, Richard—you aren't hurt, are you? You're fooling—aren't you?'

But he did not answer, and she saw that he was not fooling. He must have hit his head on the rock. She felt her heart jerk, and went down on her knees beside him, sick and frightened. It was her fault. She had challenged him. She had been stupid. The wet seaweed was dangerous. Poor old Richard!

She rolled him gently over and was horrified to see an ugly bruise on his forehead rapidly swelling to a purple lump. His left cheek was cut, bleeding.

Ever practical, Billie sprang to her feet and darted to the edge of the sea that danced and glittered in the sunlight. She dipped her handkerchief into the water, raced back to Richard, and laid the cold, wet linen on his forehead. Then he stirred and groaned.

She was very relieved. For a moment she had been terribly afraid that her foolish challenge had had serious consequences ... might have meant concussion. But he was opening his eyes now. And she was amazed to feel the sting of tears in her own.

'Oh, Richard!' she said. 'Are you all right, old thing?'

'Yes ... all right ...' he muttered. 'Damn silly of me! ... What happened?'

'You slipped and hit your head. So sorry. It was my fault,' she broke out generously.

He tried to smile, but it was a feeble effort. His temples were on fire, splitting with pain. He put a hand up to the bruise gingerly.

'Ye gods, what a bump!' he laughed weakly. 'It—it's making me feel darned sick!'

His eyes closed again. Billie's heart smote her. She looked anxiously up and down the beach. They were some way from Gale Towers, and not a soul in sight.

'Billie——' Richard muttered.

She looked down at him again—and suddenly, on a queer impulse, took one of his hands. The unexpected tenderness from her sent a thrill of wildest rapture through the veins of the man, and made him forget the pain in his head. His fingers tightened about hers.

'Billie——' he said again.

She took it that he was dazed and foolish from the pain and knock to his head—not that he was the least in love with her—and allowed him to retain her hand. At the same time she smoothed the dark hair back from his forehead. It was wet, sticky with seawater, and clung to her fingers. A slow blush crept up under her tan. She found her heart thumping in the most curious fashion. She had never felt it beat like that before. But then, never before had she stroked a man's head or held his hand. She was astonished at herself—especially at the unknown store of feeling which this man was arousing in her.

It struck her in this moment that Richard Bromley meant more to her than most people—more than she had ever intended that he should mean.

Suddenly she snatched her fingers away and stood up, jeering at herself.

'Ass!—to get soft just because he's fainted and hurt his head,' she thought. 'You'd far better do something more sensible than stroke his head, Billie Carden!'

Then she remembered that she was not Billy Carden—but Billie Bromley—and the wife of the man who lay on the sand at her feet. She began to be afraid of her own thoughts and trod upon them unmercifully.

'Look here, Richard,' she said in the old curt voice, 'I'd better run home and get Trenance to help you get——'

'Nothing of the kind,' he broke in. He struggled up and gained his feet, swaying slightly. 'I'm right as rain,' he added. 'If you'll just give me your arm, I'll get home easily.'

'Are you sure?' She frowned at him.

'Certain. I only feel a bit sick and giddy.'

'Hang on to my shoulder, then,' she said.

He looked down at her with eyes grown suddenly passionate. But she was not looking at him now. She was staring ahead of her, frowning. He sighed.

'Annoyed because I kept her hand, I suppose,' he mused. 'Oh, my dear, my dear, how futile it is—loving you!'

He put his arm around her shoulder and began to walk slowly along the beach. When they reached the door of Gale Towers, after an arduous and difficult climb up the cliff, Billie saw that Richard's face was ghastly and his brow dripping wet. She realised, with a feeling of admiration for him, that he was feeling bad but had refused to show it; forced himself to get home without any fuss.

'I'm awfully sorry about the fall, Richard,' she said kindly. 'You'd better go and lie down. I'll bring you some eau-de-Cologne for that head.'

'Thanks,' he said. 'And I'm sorry I was idiot enough to fall.'

He lay down for the rest of the afternoon with an agonising headache. But it was not the physical pain that kept him wide awake, despite the drawn blinds and eau-de-Cologne on his brow. It was the thought of Billie ... the memory of that slim hand so unexpectedly gentle, smoothing back his hair.

'If she only knew,' he thought. 'If she only knew what she meant to me ...'

Yet he was forced to realise that it was better for them both that she should never know.

She, on her part, remained downstairs with Vera and Tony, lazing about the garden in hammocks for the rest of the afternoon. But although she was careless, laughing, apparently unconcerned about her husband, she was genuinely anxious and sorry about his fall, for which she blamed herself.

She would liked to have gone up to his room once or twice to see how he was, or if she could do anything. But she could not trust herself to do it. The habit of a lifetime made her conceal her anxiety. Nevertheless she felt her heart-beats quicken when he came down to dinner that night. The bruise on his forehead had gone down a little, but he looked white and tired, and rather 'in the wars,' with a piece of sticking-plaster across the cut cheek.

'Feeling all right now?' she asked, in her direct way.

'Quite,' he said. 'I'm by no means a corpse yet.'

'I can't think how you came to do it, old man,' said Tony, with an anxious look at his brother.

'It was my fault,' said Billie. 'I challenged him to race me.'

'Nonsense. It was my own fault slipping,' said Richard.

Their eyes met. But only for the fraction of an instant. Billie quickly turned from him. And suddenly she knew quite definitely that she no longer wanted to remain at Gale Towers in constant touch with this man. Something ... something indefinable, intangible, was changing her. She was being forced by unknown quantities into dangerously soft feelings—into the kind of emotion she had always despised and ignored. Why one glance from Richard's blue, tired eyes should make her heart beat a fraction faster she did not know. She had not known why she had taken his hand on the beach when he had fainted. But this one fact was certain: she was 'going soft,' as she termed it. And that was unthinkable. She preferred to be hard and emotionless, and to be satisfied with the thrills of a fast racing car or a motor-boat, or mountain climb.

She marched to the library window and stared out of it.

'I must do something crazy, or I shall scream!' she said to herself.

CHAPTER 20

VERA watched her cousin closely during dinner. She saw all the familiar signs of restlessness in Billie. It was quite obvious to her that Billie was tired of the simple life in Tintagel, and that the adventuresome spirit in her was waking up. Vera felt amused and excited. What would she do?

After dinner, Billie announced what she meant to do.

'I've got a reckless, restless fit on,' she said curtly. 'I'm going for a moonlight spin in the racer.'

The little scarlet and silver racer had been brought down from Brighton by Billie's chauffeur. Richard had not been particularly pleased to see it. His young wife drove quite fast enough in the Vauxhall—too fast to please him. Up till now she had been too busy with the joys of the beach to do much driving. He had dreaded this moment.

'I shouldn't, if I were you, Billie,' he said.

She swung round on him—defiant at once.

'Why ever not?'

'Well, I take it you mean to do one of your seventy or eighty miles an hour stunts?' he said dryly. 'You don't know the Cornish road like I do. They are very dangerous, hilly, winding, and rough. The hedges are very high, and you can never see another car coming till it's on top of you.'

'All the more exciting,' said Billie, tossing her head.

'I repeat that I wouldn't, if I were you,' said Richard quite quietly.

Tony, who had been reading, looked up and smiled at Billie, his violet-blue eyes full of affection.

'Don't go and break you neck, dear,' he said.

'My dear old Tony, I'm a perfectly safe driver,' she said impatiently. 'Aren't I, V.?' she added, turning to her cousin.

Vera shrugged her shoulders.

'You've certainly never had a serious smash yet, but I think Richard is right about the Cornish roads—they're awful. Don't ask me to come with you.'

'I haven't asked you,' said Billie, and now she was a little white round the mouth. Vera secretly exulted. She knew Billie in this defiant, reckless mood. She could see that Richard also had a stubborn look in his eyes. What fun if these two strong wills were going to clash!

Richard, sitting in an arm-chair with his long legs stretched out, put his hand in his pocket, drew out a pipe, and knocked it against the fender.

'If you must have a moonlight scorch, take Rawlinson,' he said, in the same quiet voice.

'Poof!—no, thank you—I don't want a chauffeur,' she said. 'Good-bye, all of you. I'm off.'

Richard stared after her. Then he suddenly realised how dear, how incredibly dear, she was to him—this slender, defiant girl with her boyish brown head and hard little face. He got up and followed her into the hall.

'Billie,' he said.

'Coming?' she jeered.

'No—I'm not. I don't want to die young. Not for worlds would I go along these dangerous roads in the racer at seventy an hour. I tell you it's not safe.'

'Is one likely to meet another car? We're right out of civilisation here.'

'There are cars and carts on the road, all the same, and the moon's none too bright to-night.'

'I hate being argued with or bullied,' she said sharply. 'If I want to take the racer out, I shall do it.'

He adored her—adored her for her defiance and pride and the fearlessness of her. But he had the primitive desire to fight her—to conquer ... male over female.

'Look here, my dear,' he said, 'why do you want to be stupidly reckless? What's put you in this sort of mood?'

She did not answer. She was taking a coat down from the hall-stand and putting it over her evening-gown. Then she smiled at him grimly.

'It's quite evident you don't know me, Richard,' she said. 'I'm afraid I get these moods at times, and I won't be defeated by anything or thwarted by any one.'

'You deserve to get smashed up,' he said, with sudden heat. 'You're just a spoiled baby.'

Her mouth tightened. Her eyes became dangerously narrow and hard.

'May I ask what right you have to criticise anything that I do?'

'I quite realise I have no right—that I am only a husband by apology,' he said with sarcasm. 'On the other hand, if I saw a complete stranger in a reckless mood about to do a stupid thing, I would try to stop him.'

'Well, take my advice and only try and stop me,' she said, with a short laugh. 'I'm not used to being controlled.'

'That's evident,' he said. 'But are we quarrelling? Is it necessary, Billie?'

'Not at all, if you will kindly remember that I object to criticism or to being ordered about.'

'I'm not ordering you—only *asking* you not to go out alone in the racer on these rotten roads.'

She hesitated. She saw suddenly how weary, how pale he looked. And that was a rotten bruise on his head. Her fault, too! But scarcely had the soft feelings entered Billie's heart than she thrust them away. Her stupid softness this afternoon had put her into this restless, discontented mood, and she was not going to make it worse. Neither was she going to allow this man to make an obedient *wife* of her.

'Sorry,' she said. 'I intend to go. Good-bye.'

Richard's blood was up now. He loved her—was appalled by the vision of her speeding along the twisting Cornish roadways alone, the speedometer leaping up to seventy, even eighty miles an hour. It made him sick to think of what her end might be if she skidded, or crashed into another vehicle. In addition to this, he himself hated being defied. His temperament was not unlike her own.

'Seems to me it's a question of who's going to win this fight,' he said, biting his lips.

'It isn't even a fight,' she said coldly. 'I'm just going.'

'Billie, I ask you not to.'

She wanted to give in, to admit her folly. But not for worlds could she surrender pride and will to him—now.

She walked to the front door and opened it.

Richard marched up to her and put a hand on her arm.

'Look here,' he said angrily. 'I'm not an ordinary husband with any authority over you, I admit; but I'm sort of—sort of responsible for you while you are living with me, Billie, and I won't have you racing out in that damned car alone just because you're stubborn. You're not to do it.'

'You won't have me living with you after to-morrow,' she said in cold fury. 'I shall pack up and get out.'

His heart sank at that. He felt suddenly very miserable and helpless. But he kept his hand on her arm.

'Do what you like to-morrow,' he said. 'But you're not going to race that car to-night.'

'Oh, but I am,' said Billie. "Bye, Richard.'

She slipped from his grasp, walked to the front door and opened it. The next instant it had slammed—in Richard's face.

Then Richard lost his temper. Her cool indifference to his wishes, her disregard of his warning, her whole stubborn, wayward conduct roused him from misery to sheer rage. He marched to the door, opened it, and followed her.

She was walking swiftly down the gravel path that wound round the house to the garage of Gale Towers. It was a warm, still night, but a thin circle of yellow surrounding the moon indicated rain, and now and then a cloud darkened that pale, shining, rather lachrymose face. Richard could just see Billie, a slim dark shape in her leather motor-coat, disappearing round the bend of the Towers. He hastened after her, caught her up as she reached the one and only monkey-puzzle tree which the garden boasted, and which threw fantastic shadows on the smooth-clipped velvet of the grass. She swung round and faced him, with defiance and anger gleaming in her eyes.

'It's no use you following me, Richard. I'm going for that drive, and you can't prevent me.'

'I ask you not to, Billie.'

'No use. I'm going. I've never yet been ordered about or interfered with, and you've no right to try and domineer like this. It's not in our compact.'

'The compact can go to blazes,' said Richard, losing his last shred of self-control. 'When I made it I had no idea you would try and do utterly stupid, senseless things. I consider I have a right, under the circumstances, to stop you scorching along these dangerous roads by yourself at night.'

She gave a short, nervous laugh.

'We're wasting a lot of time over this,' she said. 'The whole argument is ridiculous, and you're making a mountain out of a mole-hill.'

'Very well, then, come along back to the house.'

'I am going for my drive, Richard.'

'Do you want me to use physical force and prevent you from going?'

'You'd better not do that,' she said in a warning voice. Her whole body had stiffened at the threat.

'Why not?' he said, breathing hard and fast. 'You pretend to be so masculine, so superior, so independent. But there's one thing you women can never have—that's the superiority of physical strength, except in a few isolated cases. I can pick you up in my arms and hold you there, my child.'

'Don't dare try,' she said.

'Are you coming back with me, sensibly?'

'No, I am not.'

'All right, then. I shall win this fight in the only way I can,' he said between set teeth.

134

He put out an arm, caught her round the waist, and with the other arm about her shoulders, swung her right off her feet and held her securely against him. She began by jeering, struggling violently.

'You won't do this for long—I'm heavy—you fool!— idiot!—*brute!* . . .' Her voice sank, rather than rose—sank to a deep note of rage, the futile rage of one who finds herself fighting against overwhelming odds. Richard was very powerful, and his arms held her like a vice. She kicked, kicked him hard on the shin once, and felt him wince with the pain. But he only laughed at her.

'Beast!—beast!' she panted. 'Put me down—put me down . . . oh, I'll make you sorry for this . . .'

He was not sorry then. He was uncontrollably angry with her and pleased with his own strength. For the moment he had forgotten his fall of the morning, his aching, bruised head. He was intent upon keeping a firm hold of the girl in his arms. Her hair was dishevelled, her face white, her eyes gleaming up at him with dark hatred, her teeth clenched.

The struggle went on silently for a couple of minutes. Once or twice Richard staggered and nearly dropped that kicking, fighting burden. Billie was not light. Although slender, she was firmly, boyishly made, and she knew how to kick hard. But the contest was an uneven one, and he won it. Suddenly she stopped struggling and went limp in his arms. He looked down at her, and she looked straight back. In that lightning glance between them passed all the anger, the defiance, the eternal and passionate warfare that exists between the sexes. The rage passed from the man, and there came upon him the full force of his love for this girl who combated him. He was in a dangerous mood, and before he knew what was happening was precipitated from passionate anger into passionate love. His arms tightened about her, he bent his head, and he spoke her name with a kind of groan.

'Billie——'

She did not answer. She was helpless, spent with her rage. Then he kissed her. It was a long kiss—born of despair as

135

well as passion—for he knew that she would neither forgive nor understand, and that after this she would go from him. But he held her motionless against him, his lips hard upon her mouth, his eyes closed, for what seemed to her an interminable time.

She was too dazed by his sudden precipitation from anger to sex-emotion to analyse her own feelings very accurately. She neither moved nor attempted to put an end to that passionate kiss. She only realised to the full his complete mastership—not only his mastership of her, but that of all men over all women—in the end. With that realisation came the bitterness of humiliation, the taste of defeat—the first defeat Billie had ever experienced in her life. She was beaten—by this man. She was not the independent boy of her own imagination. She was the woman of his. By sheer brute force he had conquered her weak femininity. Through the strength and heat of his passion, consciousness of her own sex was thrust upon her.

But the time was not yet ripe for the complete subjugation of this particular woman to this particular man, nor for her to feel pleasure or pride in his mastership. She only felt shame—shame because he had won, and because something terrifyingly urgent and new within her stirred her to respond to that kiss he was pressing upon her lips. For the third time the rememberance of her dream flashed upon her. The first time he had kissed her she had been irritated and a little afraid. But to-night she was wholly afraid, as much of her own emotions as of his. She was ashamed of the sentiments at which she had always jeered. The new woman in her bade her surrender, resign herself to her natural impulses, put her arms about his neck and say, 'I love you, Richard, and I belong to you for ever.' But the old Billie shrank from it and encased the newborn emotions in hard ice.

He, meanwhile, like one drunk with the intoxication of that kiss, suddenly grew sober. He raised his head, breathless, flushed. Then he set her down on her feet.

'Well?' he said hoarsely. 'Well, Billie—I suppose this is the end—isn't it?'

136

She did not answer for a moment. She pulled a handkerchief from her coat-pocket and passed it slowly over her lips. That mute action, so eloquent of distaste, hurt him cruelly. His colour faded. He looked suddenly very tired and haggard, and became conscious that his head ached—felt as though it were on fire.

She replaced the handkerchief in her pocket. Her young face was hard as nails. Now that she was out of his arms, she was much more confident of herself, confident that she could quite well put this man and these kind of devastating emotions right out of her life without hurting herself in the least. Her voice, however, was not quite steady as she spoke to him.

'I don't for a moment suppose you are sorry, nor have you any excuse to offer. You have simply broken our compact. Of course I can't possibly live under the same roof with you again.'

His hands clenched at his sides.

'Billie, perhaps you don't quite understand——' he began.

'I don't want to understand,' she said icily. 'Your feelings in this matter don't interest me.'

'My God—you're a heartless little——'

'I've never pretended to have a heart,' she broke in again. 'I chose to marry you because I understood you had had your experience with women, been badly let down, and didn't intend to have any more.'

'Quite so,' he said, swallowing hard. 'And I realise now that I did wrong to strike the bargain I did. Genuinely, I didn't ever think it possible that I could care for a woman again; but I was deceiving myself. I do care—much too much—for you.'

She flushed scarlet and looked down at the ground, beating a tattoo with one foot on the gravel. Her heart had given a peculiar twisting throb as she had heard his last few words. But she ignored everything save the sensation that she was being drawn into a net from which she must escape. Old prejudices, the beliefs and habits of a lifetime, are much too strong to be banished in a moment. Freedom had always meant everything to Billie. Richard Bromley stood for captivity—for the domination of her, body and mind—and she mentally fled from it.

'That's all rot!' she said.

'Thanks,' said he ironically.

'I don't believe in love, as you know,' she went on hastily. 'I liked you as a pal, but now you've chosen to break your word and be stupid, well——' She finished with a shrug of the shoulders.

He looked down at her in silence a moment. He loved her, was hungry for her love, felt a stab of sharp pain go through him at the sight of her relentless little face. He was tempted to throw himself at her feet, now, this minute; to seize her hands, pour out his love, his longing, beg for her pity, beg for one crumb of comfort. He was literally starving for her—for her tenderness, her sympathy. But he, too, was proud. He had beaten her by brute force, but the physical triumph of that had passed, leaving only the taste of ashes in his mouth. It was a poor triumph. Mentally he had not been able to touch her. He squared his shoulders, took out a cigarette, and lit it with a shaking hand.

'I quite understand,' he said. 'And I admit that I have been the one to break the compact, therefore must take the blame. And I can't hope or expect that you should ever know the meaning of love—of what I feel for you.'

'I have heard it called by another name,' she flashed, careless of hurting him, foolishly confident that she would not hurt herself.

She saw his face change, redden, then grow white again. When he spoke his voice was as frozen as her own.

'I see,' he said. 'In that case, shall we end this conversation? It's a bit chilly standing out here. I have no coat.'

A small pulse beat rather thickly in Billie's throat. She turned and walked away from him, in the direction of the garage.

'I still intend to take my drive,' she said. 'Good-night.'

CHAPTER 21

HE made no effort to detain her, swung on his heel, and walked back to the house. She unlocked the garage door without experiencing the least pleasure in the fact that she was getting her own way in the end. She knew she was being very childish and unreasonable. She also knew that she had offended Richard—cut him to the quick. And that remark of hers had been in poor taste.

'It was vile of me,' she thought. 'Small wonder if he thinks me an absolute vulgarian.'

He was not thinking that as he re-entered the house and closed the door behind him. But he was hurt, coldly furious with her. He was a sensitive man under the mask of hard cynicism which he had adopted since Olive had run away from him.

'*I have heard it called by another name . . .*' Billie had said. That rankled. It was an insult he would find hard to forgive. For it was not sheer, unadulterated passion that had led him to kiss her to-night. It was love, friendship, affection, anything save the thing she believed it.

Now he knew what she thought of him, and of all men. Now he could see the utter hopelessness of ever trying to make her care for him. It was the end, indeed. To-morrow, one of them, or both of them, would leave Gale Towers.

He walked wearily into the drawing-room and found Vera still there. The girl was half sitting, half lying on the sofa, turning over the pages of a fashion paper. She looked very pretty and charming, the lamp just behind her throwing up the bright lights in her golden hair. When Richard entered the room, she smiled at him gaily.

'Lo, Cousin Richard. Who won? Billie, I presume, since you've come back alone.'

'Yes—she won,' he said very slowly, and sat down by the window, his face turned from her, his body limp, rather huddled, in an attitude suggestive of despair.

Vera's clever little brain worked swiftly. She put down the magazine and stared across the room at him. Her heart beat very fast. She guessed there had been what she termed 'an almighty row.' That was obvious. And Billie had gone off, after all. Poor old Richard! Poor *darling* Richard! He was so handsome, so attractive. What a fool Billie was! Vera felt a longing to make this man turn his attention to her.

She rose from the sofa and came near him.

"Fraid you're tired and depressed, my dear,' she said in a honey-soft voice. 'I can guess what you feel.'

'Can you?' He gave a hard little laugh and turned a set white face to her. 'I doubt it, Vera.'

'Oh yes, I can,' she said. 'I've lived with Billie for years, and I know how worn out I used to feel after a struggle of any kind with her. She always seems to win, too—she's hard as nails.'

'Yes—she is hard.'

'I hope the quarrel hasn't been serious,' said Vera, looking down at him with grave soft eyes.

'More serious than you realise,' he said, with a dreary laugh. 'It's the finish of everything, Vera. I'm afraid you'll see the Gale Towers house-party breaking up to-morrow.'

'Oh no!' said Vera. 'Oh no, Richard; you don't mean that, do you?'

'I do,' he said.

'But why?'

'I can't very well explain.'

'Yes, you can,' said Vera. 'I'd understand. Tell me, Richard—let me help if you can.'

'You're kind,' he said shortly. 'But you couldn't possibly help. Nobody can.'

Vera threw him an interrogating glance. She was flushed

and her eyes were brilliant with excitement. This was the moment she had watched for, awaited. Richard and Billie had had a serious quarrel and were going to separate. This was the hour in which Vera hoped to catch Richard's heart on the rebound. She set herself out to be sweetly sympathetic and wholly understanding of the case. She had never been sweeter, kinder, more attractive. Richard was desperately unhappy and humiliated. He was only human, and the balm of Vera's sympathy was momentarily desirable to him.

She had pulled a big silk hassock up to his chair and curled up on it at his feet. He thought, as he looked down at her, how different she was from Billie. She was so essentially feminine and soft. She was very pretty, too, with that flushed, ardent face and bright gold hair; her neck looked lily-white through the thin black lace of the dinner-frock she was wearing. The dress had one great cluster of scarlet flowers on the left hip—matching the artificial scarlet of her lips. She was looking up at him with an expression of great concern.

'Oh, Cousin Richard, I'm so sorry—you look so miserable. Can't you tell me what has happened?'

'Not very well.'

'Is it—is it that you—care for Billie?'

He was too raw to admit it, could not discuss Billie. He kept silence. But Vera saw his hand clench and unclench, and knew the answer. It was just what she had thought.

'Don't tell me anything, then,' she said in a low murmur. 'You needn't. I can guess. I'm terribly sorry. I hoped you would—be happy.'

'Not a hope of that. But she seems to be happy, so what's it matter? To-morrow I shall kick out and get a job. It serves me right for ever marrying under such conditions,' he said harshly.

'But it does matter—to me,' Vera said, her breath quickening. 'I *wanted* you to be happy.'

He stared at her.

'I don't see why, my dear child.'

141

'No—of course you don't,' she whispered. And now her lashes drooped and her cheeks grew carmine, and the golden head was bowed with a pretty suggestion of shyness and shame.

Richard frowned. He was experienced enough with women to realise what this girl suggested. But he was also too experienced to trust or believe in her.

'It's nice of you to mind whether I'm happy or not,' he said shortly. 'But I assure you it doesn't matter. The only regret I have is for Tony. He has been happy here, poor old chap.'

'I'm much more upset for your sake than Tony's. Oh, really I am!' Vera declared, raising her head and looking up at him. 'Richard, can't I do anything to help?'

'Nothing.'

'Must you and Billie separate?'

'Absolutely essential.'

'Where will you go? What will you do?'

'I haven't the least idea. One can't decide these things in a moment.'

'I—see,' said Vera slowly.

Her heart was sinking. Shallow, vain though she was, she at present laboured under the delusion that she cared for Richard Bromley. She was of the nature and type that demands a sentimental affair of some kind; more often than not wallows in an emotional regard for the one person who ignores her. Her vanity was piqued by Richard's lack of interest in her beauty and charm. It was far from her intention to marry and settle down with a penniless man, and Richard, apart from the money he obtained as Billie's husband, was penniless. But she was willing and eager to plunge into an *affaire de cœur*. It was contrary to her scheming that he should just disappear into the void, where she could not see or attempt to console him.

She possessed a fair amount of nerve, of belief that it pays to take the bull by the horns. She managed to squeeze real, big tears into her eyes, and a half-sob into her voice when she next spoke to Richard.

'Oh, I don't want you to go—I don't want this house-party to break up!'

'Well, it will,' said Richard grimly.

'I don't mind about the others,' she said recklessly. 'But I don't want *you* to go away!'

His heart have an uncomfortable throb. He threw her a hasty glance, saw her blue eyes ardent, swimming in tears, fixed upon him—her hands clasped to her breast. It had never struck him that Vera would mind whether he lived or died. He had thought her a pretty, vain, fashionable product of the day, but had never endowed her in his imagination with any real feeling or depth of character.

Was she trying to tell him that she was in love with him? If so, it was extremely awkward. It embarrassed him beyond words. He was not attracted by her, any more than any mere male man is attracted by an undeniably pretty girl. While he sat there, ruminating, rather anxiously surveying her, she made up her mind to go 'full steam ahead' while she was in a desperate mood. She covered her face with her hands.

'Now what will you think of me?' she moaned. 'Oh, Richard, it's all such a tangle . . . you're a fool about Billie . . . and I'm being a fool about you!'

'My dear child!' he protested.

'Yes,' she said, 'yes! I can't bear to see you so unhappy and lonely—because I care—I care what becomes of you!'

The hardness of his mouth and eyes relaxed a little. But he was still horribly embarrassed, and incredulous of her sincerity.

'My dear,' he repeated. 'Please don't—it's sweet of you, but I—you see——'

'Oh, I expect you to despise me for letting you see how I feel!' she broke in, raising her face and gazing up at him, scarlet, tearful; quite aware that she looked charming, like a crestfallen, golden-haired nymph. 'But I'm not ashamed. I'm proud of my feelings for you, Richard. You're so wonderful—the most wonderful man I've ever known.'

'Oh, my dear little girl, for goodness' sake——'

'Let me help you—let me be of some use,' she went on in a passionate voice. 'I'm not hard like Billie. I understand human nature. I know what it is to feel desperate and broken-hearted. I do, I do now. Oh, Richard——'

She had bowed her head on his knees. He was not roused by her passion, but stirred to natural pity by her pretty appeal. He, who understood so well the misery and heart-break of hopeless love, could afford to be sorry for her if she was sincere, if she really cared. But he had never dreamed . . . it was most awkward . . . difficult . . . he looked down at the golden head on his knee and then instinctively put an arm around her.

'Poor child!' he said.

It was at that precise instant that Billie opened the drawing-room door and marched into the room.

Billie had not gone for her drive after all. She had sat down in the garage on the footboard of the car, smoked a cigarette in peace and quiet, and returned to saner mood. Having reviewed the angry, passionate scene she had just had with her husband, she had definitely decided she must part from him before she weakened in the resolve. But she had also decided that she had insulted him unnecessarily. It was quite possible he did care for her with sincere affection, and, if so, she had no right to accuse him of baser kind of emotion.

It was rarely that Billie apologised to anybody. But she had made up her mind to apologise to Richard for that insult which she had flung at him, even though they never met again.

It was unfortunate for Richard that she should have come upon this fresh scene which Vera was enacting. The sight of Richard, with his arm around Vera and Vera's golden head on his knees, robbed Billie of any desire to beg Richard's pardon. She now felt justified in what she had said. He had said he loved her, kissed her in the most passionate manner; and here he was, ten minutes later, consoling himself with Vera!

Richard, when he saw his wife in the doorway, sprang to

his feet, and Vera hastily gained hers. She felt rather guilty and embarrassed. Richard was the latter, without being in the least the former. Billie's grey-green eyes met his in a look that was coldly contemptuous.

'Don't let me interrupt, you two,' she said, in a tone of deep disdain. 'It was quite a pretty picture.'

Vera said nothing. Her heart was galloping. She had felt Richard's arm about her. That seemed to her foolish mind the first stage in his downfall. But she was very wrong. A second ago he had pitied her. Now, with Billie in the room making contemptuous and acid remarks, he was pitiless, furious that he should have been put into such an invidious position. Billie had altogether an erroneous idea of things.

'It was not a pretty picture at all,' he snapped.

She deliberately yawned.

'It doesn't interest me, anyhow. Good-night. I'm off to bed. I'm too tired to take that drive.'

'Wait,' said Richard. 'Don't go. I want to speak to you.'

'The morning will do,' she said. 'I'm tired now. Good-night. Good-night, Vera.'

She walked straight out of the room again and up the stairs. As she passed between the two armoured, visored knights, she felt childish irritation, and struck at them both, making a little chink on the cold, hard armour with her nails.

'Idiotic things!' she muttered.

Up in her bedroom she stood before the open window and stared at the night, letting the cool breeze play on her hot cheeks. The moon was entirely hidden by clouds, and she could hear the soft patter of rain on the trees. There was no wind, no storm. The sea was unusually quiet, the eternal surge of it muffled by the falling summer rain. Somewhere near Gale Towers an owl hooted, twice. Then silence again.

Billie had run a veritable gamut of emotions to-night. She swung now from anger and defiance to something quite foreign to her—sheer feminine jealousy. With hands doubled at her sides, she stared out of the window, visualising that scene she had unexpectedly come upon.

Vera, at Richard's knees, his arm around her! She did not know what had happened between those two—in all probability nothing serious. But what she had argued and imagined true for so long had been proven to her. Men were brute beasts. In nine cases out of ten, 'love' was passion. Richard was consoling himself with Vera. Vera was a sentimental little fool, only too ready to console him. Never, never now would she, Billie, let Richard know that she had come in to apologise to him.

But she was jealous. A new, sharp pang had stabbed her heart at the sight of Richard embracing Vera. It stabbed her now at the remembrance. She felt in some way cheated and humiliated, although she had no right to feel either. She had refused Richard Bromley's love—fled from his passion. He was independent of her. He could make love to any woman he wanted. Why should she care? But all the same she *did* care. She resented the fact that he should go straight from her to the consoling arms of Vera.

Inconsistent woman! Heaven alone knew what might have happened had Billie come in to Richard this night in her chastened mood, found him alone, and begged his pardon for insulting him! Despite all her strength and stubbornness, she might have given way, had he pleaded afresh—yielded to her natural impulses at last. She had always liked and admired him. It would not have taken much to conquer completely that wayward, boyish heart of hers.

But now the pendulum swung back again. She was the old, cynical, hard Billie. She trod upon her jealousy with merciless footsteps, ashamed of it, denying it.

'I don't care a hang—let him divorce me and marry her—I don't care—I'd rather give up my money and be free again—much rather!'

She turned from the window, marched to her dressing-table, began to undress, lips quivering, eyes furious and bright. Then suddenly, like a child, she crumpled up, flung herself on her bed, and began to cry.

Downstairs Richard was very definitely putting an end to

146

his would-be consoler, thereby annoying that young woman beyond words.

'Billie has probably got the wrong idea of things altogether now,' he had said shortly, after Billie's departure. 'It's damnable, Vera.'

She came near him again and put out her hands.

'Don't let it worry you, Richard; she doesn't care—but I do.'

'Come, Vera, this is all absurd.'

'It isn't absurd. Oh, Richard, you must believe that I love you!' she said recklessly.

'You mustn't say these things—you'll be sorry for them one day, my dear little girl. I was sorry for you just now, and still am; but there can't be any sentiment of this kind between us, and you must understand that. I love Billie, and always shall.'

Vera began really to sob now—baffled and annoyed.

'Billie will never care for you or any man. Why can't you forget her?—let me help you to forget.'

'One doesn't forget so easily when one really cares. Now, Vera, for Heaven's sake, stop crying and let's be friends!'

'No,' she said hysterically. 'I can't look on you as a friend, Richard.'

'Rubbish. I'm years older than you are, and twice a married man,' he said, with a short, bitter laugh. 'But you won't be called upon to suffer me even as a friend, my poor child, as I'm off first thing in the morning. Buck up—get a grip of yourself—and shake hands. It's all rather absurd, and what happened just now has done me more harm than you know. Pull yourself together, Vera.'

She refused to stop crying or to shake hands. After a moment, exasperated and tired out, Richard left her. He could not deal with hysteria and what he felt certain was a foolish infatuation which she would speedily get over. Much more serious things had happened to him. He loved Billie, his wife, and to-morrow he would be separating from her for ever. He felt almost broken.

He paused for a moment outside Billie's bedroom door. With his heart furiously shaking, he called her name:

'Billie!'

The answer came at once—cold—brusque:

'Yes, what is it?'

'Billie, I must speak to you.'

'Not now. I'm in bed.'

'Please,' he said in a low, pleading voice. 'There is so much to be said, and I can't wait until to-morrow.'

Silence for a moment. He held his breath, cursing his own stupidity because his forehead was wet and his hands trembling. Could he have seen through that door he would have witnessed a Billie who was far from cool or self-confident. She was sitting up in bed, knees hunched, hands locked about them, a very hot, flushed face turned in his direction. Her eyes were red with weeping. She was miserable, wretched, because the whole thing had happened to destroy the happiness of the life which had been so pleasant, so peaceful down here this summer. But she was much too proud to let Richard see how miserable she was, and she hardened her heart against that voice which pleaded outside her door. If he imagined she would welcome him, after his philandering with Vera, he was wrong, she reflected.

'Billie,' he called urgently. 'Won't you come and talk to me? I don't want to go to bed without explaining—you misunderstood—I——'

'Please leave me alone,' she broke in. 'There is nothing to explain, and I don't misunderstand.'

'But you do!'

'Good-night, Richard,' she said in that hard little voice.

He shrugged his shoulders and moved away with a bitter look in his handsome eyes.

'She's absolutely heartless and dead against me now. I might as well try to get blood out of a stone,' he thought dejectedly.

How was he to know that she felt as unhappy as himself? That after the sound of his footsteps had died away and she heard his bedroom door shut, she relaxed her muscles, flung herself face downward on the pillows again, slender body quivering. Vera tried to gain an audience from her cousin that night, but was not admitted. Billie did not even answer the knock. She pretened to be asleep. But she did not go to sleep for a long, long while. She could not forget all that had happened to-day—Richard's accident on the seashore this morning when he had fainted, after slipping on that dangerous rock—the memory of her own anxiety and remorse for challenging him—the way his fingers had clung to hers in his dazed, suffering state. Then again the quarrel to-night and the subsequent scene out in the garden. Once more she lived through that passionate embrace, that long, breathless kiss he had laid on her lips; the confession of love for her which he had blurted out; the misery of his voice when he had said, 'I suppose this is the end!'

Yet if he had really cared, how could he have gone straight into the house and caressed Vera? That rankled in Billie's mind, and drove the softer, more regretful feelings from her as soon as they came.

No! It would not do to give way to softness. Better far to be her old hard, practical self. Had she not said to Richard when she had first met him that she had no use for love—no belief in it—that she realised it only led to disaster and unhappiness? At that time, he, too, had shared her beliefs and laughed at love; he had fallen in with all her views; seemed the one and only person who could marry her and remain her friend.

It was all over. He had changed; broken his compact. It was rather bitter to her to remember that people like Lady Jo and Vera had warned her that he would do so. They understood men better than she did. It hurt ... because she had championed Richard and put her faith in him.

And what about herself? She was slow to admit it, even in the silence and darkness of that night, during her painful soliloquy—but she had lost faith in herself. She had been through flashes of softness, of terrifying consciousness of sex

149

and natural emotions. She knew now that there were flaws in the armour of cold steel in which she had encased herself. And she was frightened lest Richard or any man in future should discover those flaws and through them destroy her. For it verily seemed to Billie that the mastership of a man would mean her destruction. She had yet to learn that in the arms of her true lover woman seeks defeat, and through her own destruction gains her most glorious victory.

While she spent most of the night worrying, regretting, steeling herself for the morrow's contest, the man she had married did not even bother to undress and go to bed. He was too tired and too miserable to sleep. The bruise on his forehead ached and throbbed. But the ache in his heart was sharper and more difficult to bear.

Richard had his regrets that night—regrets not only that he had allowed himself to fall in love and suffer all over again—but that he had ever encountered Billie. It was all so different from the affair with Olive. Olive was the ordinary, pretty, fluffy type of woman a man could forget. But Billie was a girl a man could never forget—she was so utterly original—so elusive—so heart-breakingly beyond a man's reach.

He sat up in a chair, shoulders drooping, head between his hands, listening to the grandfather-clock downstairs strike the hours, one after another. He regarded himself and his life as failure. Why he had failed in everything, he did not know. It was not for want of endeavour or courage. But he had failed! First in his business. That had been the fault of a dishonest partner. But it had failed. Then with Olive. She had been the one to go, to desert her post . . . but it must have been his fault, somewhere. At any rate, he had not been sufficiently a success as a married man to keep her. Now, in his second, extraordinary marriage, he had failed. And this time it was entirely his fault. He had let sentiment, passionate emotion, master him and put an end to the most perfect friendship he had ever known.

What now? The breaking up of everything—his separation, probably divorce, from Billie—then to begin life all over again. Richard groaned as he surveyed himself in the midst of the ruin and saw himself the complete failure. But his was not the nature to lie shattered and crushed for long. Before dawn broke over Gale Towers, he had gathered himself together and formed new resolves, firmly determined to shut this period of his career right out. For if he did not, if he just caved in before the blow of losing Billie, he would prove himself a coward as well as a failure. There was Tony to consider. For Tony's sake he must not altogether fail. He must try to forget his love for Billie, even though it had shaken the foundation of existence for him. He must be as cool, as calm, as determined as herself to-morrow, when he faced her to say good-bye. And after that, work ... work ... whatever sort of work he could procure. By working he would regain his courage and his grip upon life. He had no right to Silas Carden's money, and it was as well he should give it up. Too much idling made a man soft. But he would never be soft again.

CHAPTER 22

SO far as Tony was concerned, breakfast that next morning at Gale Towers began in the ordinary happy fashion. The big gong boomed through the house at nine o'clock, punctiliously and punctually sounded by old Trenance.

Tony and Vera were down first. The boy was in the bright and cheerful state habitual to him since his marvellous recovery to health and strength. He now walked on one stick only, was tanned to the roots of his curly hair, and a good inch taller than he had been during the old, painful, bitter days in Storrington.

He greeted Vera with a cheerful remark about the weather.

'Been raining most of the night, but it's going to clear up, isn't it, V.?'

Vera muttered an unintelligible reply. She was in a bad temper, and her pretty face was sullen and downcast. She had had ample time for reflection during the night, and like the other two had spent most of it thinking. But her thoughts had been unpleasantly ashamed. It was not agreeable to her to remember that her attempts to console Richard had ignominiously failed.

Tony was not abashed by her gloom. With the brutal frankness of extreme youth, he accused her of having a liver.

'You're yawning, and you're pale, and I'll bet you can see black specks, V. Try Kruschen and jump over the chairs with me after break——'

'Oh, be quiet, Tony,' interrupted Vera angrily.

She came to the definite conclusion that young Anthony Bromley was a hateful boy.

Tony grinned more broadly than ever, sat down, and commenced his breakfast. But when his brother and young sister-in-law joined them, he was forced to the awkward sensation that something was wrong, not only with Vera, but with everybody. And a 'liver' could not account for Richard's grim face or Billie's silence. Tony knew that set look on his brother's face. It had been there—a tight, hard look about the eyes and mouth—frequently, after Olive had run away. But Tony had not seen it for some months—certainly not since he had come down to Tintagel. It worried him. And what was wrong with Billie, who usually ate an enormous breakfast with a healthy appetite most women would envy her, and chatted gaily of bathing or golf or motoring?

The atmosphere was very strained. By the time the meal ended, complete silence reigned in the big baronial dining-room. Richard buried himself in a morning paper, and Billie and Vera exchanged not a single word beyond 'May I have the salt?' or 'Pass along the butter.'

Tony anxiously surveyed the three gloomy, silent figures, then plunged tactlessly into a leading question:

'I say, what the dickens is wrong? Anybody'd think we were just off to a funeral.'

Billie looked at him, then hastily looked away again. Richard ignored the question and asked the butler for a cigarette.

Tony's brows met in a puzzled frown.

'Something's gone wrong,' he reflected. 'Surely old Dick and Billie haven't had a row!'

He hoped not. It would remind him much too painfully of the distressing rows Richard had once had with Olive. But Billie was not a selfish little fool like Olive—a fellow could argue sensibly with Billie—meet her on his own ground. Tony cheered himself up with this reflection, and departed through the French windows on to the lawn. It was a warm, hazy morning, and the sun was just struggling through a feathery mass of white cloud. It was going to be a fine day.

Vera felt certain that she was not wanted by either Richard or Billie. With the same sullen look on her face, she rose and marched out of the room. She went up to her bedroom. She was not in the mood to join that facetious boy in the garden.

Richard and Billie, left alone, suddenly exchanged glances. It was a hasty look—but sufficient to show each the set, purposeful expression of the other. They were both well armoured this morning.

Richard was the first to speak. With his eyes carefully fixed on the cigarette he had just lighted he said:

'Last night, Billie, I intended to try and explain what—what you saw when you came into the drawing-room and found me with my arm around Vera. But this morning I shall not attempt to make any explanations or excuses. I merely wish to inform you that when I leave Gale Towers to-day, I shall not be seeing your cousin again—in case you imagine I intend to ruin her young life.'

The sarcastic voice stung the colour into Billie's cheeks,

and reminded her queerly of the Richard she had first met at Storrington.

'I don't imagine that at all,' she said. 'But anyhow it does not really matter to me whether you see Vera again or not. You say "when you leave Gale Towers to-day." Am I to understand you are going to-day, then?'

'Yes,' he said. 'One of us must go, and it is my place to quit. Gale Towers is for the moment your property and not mine. I shall go, and take Tony with me.'

Her heart gave a queer jerk. She threw him a swift look, but he was not looking at her. He was still staring intently at his cigarette. He was obviously very tired. The bruise on his forehead was an ugly purple, and there were dark lines under his eyes. But it struck her even then that the shape of his head was remarkably fine, and that he was the best-looking man she had ever known.

'I didn't intend you to go,' she said, after a pause.

'Why not?'

'Well—I—I meant to go myself. In fact, I shall.'

'No need for both of us to go.'

'What do you think I should find to do here alone with Vera?' she flashed.

'Oh, well'—he shrugged his shoulders—'we had better both go. After last night'—a muscle in his throat worked—'I can't possibly remain here and take your uncle's money. I intend to look for work at once.'

'For work!' she repeated, frowning.

'Certainly. It is my ambition to pay back every penny you have spent on Tony or myself.'

That cut her. She rose and began to walk up and down the dinning-room. She wore a straight-cut grey costume and silk shirt and tie. Richard, with a covert glance at her, knew that he must always remember her like this ... the boyish Billie, with hands thrust in her pockets and that tie, of her favourite green shade, throwing up the green light in her bright, fine eyes. But he would have died now sooner than give way to sentiment. He looked away from her—stiff, cold, immovable. It was she who was the more disturbed of the two this morning.

'You needn't think I regret anything I did for Tony—or for you,' she said at last, with difficulty. 'I shall not take a penny back.'

'It will be placed at your bank to your credit,' he said.

'If you feel like that, very well,' she said, biting her lower lip. 'But look here, Richard—there's one important fact to face which we are both forgetting. Uncle Silas—and the money.'

'Yes,' said Richard. 'I haven't forgotten it.'

'You quite realise that all our trouble, our acting, that ridiculous marriage, have been for nothing? Uncle Silas is no fool, and when he hears we have separated he will rush across the water to find out what is wrong, attempt to reunite us, then see for himself that we never were an ordinary couple, and that he has been tricked.'

Richard smoked hard for a moment.

'Yes, I see that,' he said at length. 'Which means, I presume, that he will be furiously angry and disinherit you on the spot—or order you to divorce me instantly and marry again.'

Her cheeks flamed.

'I shouldn't dream of doing that!'

'No—I dare say once has been quite enough,' he said sarcastically.

She felt more uncomfortable and uncertain of herself than she had ever felt in her life. Somehow, despite her armour-plating, she was being hurt by this man, made to feel thoroughly wretched. She had not been at all unhappy in her brief married life—till last night. She had enjoyed it— enjoyed every minute of her companionship with Richard Bromley. He was a more interesting, agreeable friend than any woman with whom she had associated. Her mind fled back to the memory of their drives, their walks, their mutual enjoyment of Nature; their common tastes in little ordinary everyday things. They had been really perfect 'pals.' How could she maintain otherwise? It was only last night that had spoiled everything.

'Richard, don't let us mistake one another,' she said, her brows contracted. She ceased her restless pacing and stood before him, smooth brown head lowered, gaze concentrated on a patch of sunlight that threw up the rich red of the Turkey rug at her feet. 'So long as we were—good friends—I—I did not mind our marriage.'

'Thanks,' he said in the same dry tone. 'But on the other hand, you never wanted to marry me, which I quite understand. And you can't possibly ever want to repeat the experience, now you know what brutes we men are.'

'Must you be so sarcastic?' she flashed, with indignation.

He gave an unhappy laugh.

'I apologise. But naturally I feel rather like a bear with a sore head this morning. No—don't bother to remind me it's my own fault—I know that. Now, shall we come to hard facts? If we separate, Mr. Carden will find out that he has been tricked, and take your money away from you. If you want to keep it, and I can do anything to help you, I will; because you have been so kind to Tony. He owes his health, his life, practically to you, and I shall never forget that.'

'I don't want you to be grateful or to feel under any obligation,' she said earnestly. 'I'm fond of the boy, and only too glad I was able to help him.'

'Thank you,' he said, this time without sarcasm. 'As far as finance is concerned, you are the most generous person in the world.'

'But ungenerous in other things, eh?' she said, with a nervous little laugh, her colour coming and going.

'Let's keep off the personal,' he said. 'It's better. What conclusion have you come to about the future?'

She was a little surprised and baffled by his new steely manner. Of course she preferred it to an emotional outburst. She was too afraid of herself to want that. On the other hand, she was curiously piqued because he seemed so indifferent and hard—so ready to leave her for good. She held her head erect and met steel with steel.

'Only that we can't go on with this farse of living as man and wife here—or anywhere.'

'The so-called honeymoon must come to an abrupt end.'

'Yes,' she greed. 'But Uncle Silas——'

'He'll have to know, of course. He writes to you here and expects long, graphic descriptions of our doings. But if you wish to go on deceiving him, and to keep your money, why not pretend we have gone abroad?'

'That couldn't last,' said Billie slowly. 'There's bound to be a time when he'd see through that. No—I had better give up the money. I ought to have done so in the first place.'

'I don't wish to be the cause of your losing your money if I can help you keep it,' said Richard, in a worried way. 'On the other hand, I'm afraid I've already spoiled things.'

She visualised the immediate future apart from him: herself wandering about the Continent, or returning to her Brighton bungalow, or giving up her money and having to work. Her heart sank. It was not a cheerful prospect. What was more, she knew full well that she would miss this man; that she had come to rely on his companionship. She twisted the platinum wedding-ring round her finger, her heart beating painfully fast. Then suddenly she looked at him, her face burning, and stammered out:

'Look here, it's all so silly—can't we—go back to the old footing—couldn't you——'

'No—I could not,' he broke in very coldly and decisively. 'It would be quite impossible for me to begin again or make any more compacts and break them. You don't understand—you never will—but I just can't do it. I am grateful to you, all the same, for giving me the opportunity.'

Scarlet and confused, she walked to the open windows and flung her cigarette-end on to the lawn. It was not that she did not understand—only that she did not *want to*. But she saw now that friendly happiness between them was over for ever. Suddenly, to his immense astonishment and dismay, she burst into tears.

He stared at her, dumb, motionless. The sight of Billie, the hard, the cold, the unsentimental, crying just as he might have expected any ordinary woman to cry under the circumstances, distressed him horribly. He had an insane desire to get up and catch her in his arms, tell her he adored her, comfort her, kiss the tears from her eyes. But he restrained that impulse. His all-night vigil had ended in resolutions not easily to be forgotten or broken. He was well under control this morning. He merely got up and walked to her side, laid a hand on her shoulder.

'Don't upset yourself, Billie,' he said quietly. 'Just let's talk it out quietly and reasonably. We've got to separate, but at least let us do so pleasantly. I assure you I will do all I can to make things easy. I'm quite willing to pretend to be the faithless brute of a husband who deserts you in the middle of the very honeymoon, and to give you all the necessary grounds for divorce. Then your uncle will be entirely on your side, curse my memory, and let you keep your money. How about that for a suggestion?'

With a handkerchief pressed to her lips, she listened to him. It was a generous offer, and certainly a way out through which she could retain her fortune and not suffer. But she knew definitely that she could not and would not allow this man to make such a sacrifice, to let Uncle Silas and the world regard him as a cad, a rotter which he was not, and never had been. It was unthinkable. All the same, it was wonderfully decent of him to make the offer. And suddenly she had the most astonishing feeling that, if she could only bring herself to turn round and throw herself into his arms, she would end the whole argument and save an immense amount of trouble. For an instant she stood there, quivering under the touch of his hand.

If only Richard could have seen into Billie's heart then—seized the golden moment—gathered her into his arms— there is little doubt that she would have told him to keep her there and take her, in spite of herself.

But he only let his hand rest on her shoulder a brief space, then moved away from her, his face grim.

'Well, Billie—will you do what I suggest?'

She drew a sharp breath, dabbed at her eyes fiercely with the handkerchief, ashamed of her tears. Then she faced him, once more composed, but very white.

'No—I will not. It is unnecessarily melodramatic. You haven't been a rotten, caddish sort of fellow like that, and I don't see why Uncle Silas should be made to imagine so.'

Richard took out his cigarette-case and regarded it thoughtfully.

'It doesn't much matter. And if you want a divorce——'

'No,' she broke in. 'It all sounds too beastly. Look here, Richard, let's stay married. I don't care two hoots whether I call myself Miss Carden or Mrs. Bromley—it's all the same to me so long as we are not scrapping. I'm all for a peaceful life.'

'And I,' he said, with a short laugh.

'Then we'll just live apart, which is, after all, what I said we would do once my uncle went back to America, and he will probably never find out anything. It's a much better idea, and will save a lot of bother. It seems a pity to muck up things now we've carried our scheme through so far.'

He frowned as he lit his cigarette.

'I'm game to do anything you suggest whereby you will keep your money and live in peace,' he said. 'But one thing is impossible—that is for me to take your money.'

'It isn't mine—it's what Uncle Silas settled on you.'

'Well, let it go on settling,' he said grimly. 'It can accumulate in the bank and become yours when I die. Meanwhile I intend to work and earn my own.'

'You're set on that?'

'Quite.'

She began to pace the room again. Her emotional outburst had passed completely. She was quiet and self-confident again. But the look in her eyes when she glanced at this man whom she had married was one of sincere admiration. After all, how could she help admiring him for his pride and independence after what had taken place between them!

'Very well, Richard,' she said. 'Let it rest like that. We'll go on with our supposed married life—apart—and you shall earn your living. But I intend to go on doing things for Tony.'

Richard flushed and raised his brows.

'You are very kind, Billie, but I'd rather look after the young 'un myself. It's my job.'

'No—it's mine. You see, I rather regard Tony as my protégé. You say he owes his life to me. Very well—he shall repay it by letting me look after him in the future till he's old enough to strike out on his own.'

Richard's vivid blue eyes softened.

'You're awfully decent about Tony,' he said. 'But why——?'

'Oh, I must have something to do—some object in life!' she broke in impatiently. 'Looking after my brother-in-law will amuse me.'

'Since you put it like that, I give in,' he said. 'Now, to return to the subject of myself, I shall leave Gale Towers by the midday train, go straight up to town, and look round for a job.'

She gave a nervous little laugh, walked to the window, and stared out. The haze was vanishing, and the great shining stretch of sea lay like rippling emerald silk under the sunshine. Fleecy white clouds scudded merrily across a blue sky, chased by a strong ocean breeze. A glorious, invigorating morning. The tide was out and the sands were untrodden gold; the rocks wet and glistening. Just the morning for a swim, for a race over that wide, deserted beach. In the ordinary way the little party from Gale Towers would already be climbing down the cliff-side, swimming costumes and towels over their arms. With almost painful vividness, Billie could see Richard, tall and straight, with bronzed muscular arms crossed on his chest, and blue eyes laughing at her, jeering because she yelled boyishly at the stinging coldness of the first plunge into the waves.

It had been such good fun. Richard had been such a

sportsman. And it was all over. That same merry little party would never go down to the sea-shore, laughing and joking, again.

'Oh, *damn!*' said Billie, under her breath, and bit her lower lip very hard indeed.

'You must do just what you want;' Richard was saying. 'Why not stay down here for a bit longer?'

She shrugged her shoulders and stared past him. She did not particularly want to do anything now; did not care whether she left Cornwall or returned to town.

'Oh, perhaps I will,' she said gloomily. 'It would be a pity to drag Tony away from the sea. It's doing him so much good, and Vera can either stay here or go away—as she likes.'

Richard remained silent on the subject of Vera. The thought of the girl embarrassed rather than stirred him. He grew hot at the memory of her last night, throwing herself into his arms. He would be glad to see the last of Vera.

'Right you are,' he said. 'Well, I'll get along and pack.'

'What shall I—shall we say to—the others?'

'Vera has been in the "know" all along, so tell her the truth,' he said, looking straight into her eyes now. 'Tony is more difficult.'

'Yes—he's the sentimentalist,' said Billie.

'Oh, to keep him happy, say I've got urgent business on your behalf in town. Sooner or later, I shall have to tell him the truth. Well, that's settled, Billie. The future must take care of itself. At the moment my way is clear. I'm off to town.'

She looked after him. He was walking from the room. She wanted to call out: 'Stop—don't go—it's all so stupid...' But no words came. It was futile. He had said he could not possibly remain. Much better to keep quiet and let him go.

'Oh, *damn!*' Billie repeated miserably to herself. 'Why did he spoil everything last night? What is love but trouble...? I knew it—I knew it!'

The next two hours were very difficult. Vera understood

what was happening, and was sulky and silent. But Tony was quite upset. It was 'all rot,' he said, for a fellow to have to go away on business in the middle of his honeymoon, and 'jolly hard luck.' He sympathised with his brother and sister-in-law until they both felt sick and ashamed of the lie they were acting. Finally, both Richard and Billie were strung up to an acute state of nerves. In consequence they became very short with each other. Richard withdrew deeper than ever into his new shell of cold reserve and control, and Billie always grew dumb and helpless when she was distressed. She was forced to admit to herself that she was considerably distressed when at length the time came for Richard to depart. For the sake of appearances before Tony, she volunteered to drive Richard to Camelford to catch the London express, although she would have given a great deal to avoid a farewell scene. She was relieved, however, to find her husband cool and undisturbed to the end. He asked her not to wait for the train to come in.

'I should get along back to Tintagel if I were you,' he said.

She stared at him, half resentfully. He ought to be in his old flannels and sweater, not in that smart town suit and soft hat. And he was going to look for work—to stifle in midsummer—in some cheap London hotel.

'Look here, Richard, I shan't stay at Gale Towers long—I shall come back to town myself, soon,' she broke out.

'You are your own mistress,' he said.

There were a good many things she wanted to say, but she could not voice any of her thoughts. They were too bewildering to herself. So she thrust out a hand in the old direct, boyish way.

'Good-bye, Richard,' she said. 'And let's cut out what happened and—and be quite good friends if—if we happen to meet.'

The grip of her small, strong fingers about his and the strangely forlorn look on her face very nearly broke through his reserve. He did not understand that look, but undoubtedly she was upset. He experienced the most poignant desire to take his suit-cases from the idiotic-looking porter who stood at a distance, gaping at them, fling them back into Billie's car, and tell her to drive him back to Gale Towers, to begin all over again. He was going to miss her horribly, to loathe looking for a job, alone and depressed in some hateful hotel. And he loved her ... God knew how much he loved her ... how passionately he needed her love. His hand tightened over hers with a grip that was painful. He took a long, lingering survey of her dear, boyish, sun-browned face, her bright, greenish eyes, smooth brown head under the familiar small felt hat jammed down over her brows.

When would they ever meet again? Perhaps never! Perhaps for both their sakes it would be better if he kept away from her; because he could not be the friend she demanded, he could not help being her lover. The mere fact that she bore his name, wore his ring, counted for nothing—nothing at all.

He dropped her hand and turned his face from her so that she might not see how he suffered.

'Good-bye, my child,' he said abruptly. 'Sorry I messed things up and failed you. Take care of yourself and—be happy. And I need hardly say that if ever you want me for anything. I shall be ready. Good-bye.'

She felt that she was dismissed. She turned and marched down the platform away from him and out to the waiting car. She took her place at the wheel, mechanically switched on the engine, threw in the gear, and started off. But she scarcely saw the white, dusty country road down which she was speeding. For the second time within a few hours, Billie was crying—great, hot tears that stung her eyes and blinded her sight. And something inside her seemed to be aching, hurting ... an incredible pain she had never felt in her life before.

Why she cried and why she felt that heartache, she scarcely understood. She only knew that Richard had gone, probably for good, and that she was going to know what it was to be lonely—she, the independent one who had jeered at people who rely on other folk for their happiness or peace of mind. She was going to miss Richard. She was missing him already. And it was her fault as much as his that he had gone. She had insulted him and shown him plainly that she did not want the love he had offered. Vera ... she was no longer jealous of Vera. Obviously he had no real regard for her, otherwise he would not have said good-bye to her in the brusque, cold fashion she had witnessed back at the Towers. Billie was sorry now that she had been so rude, and had refused to listen to his explanation. She was sorry for a good many things.

Forlornly Billie brushed the tears from her eyes and pressed her foot down on the accelerator. She felt she must go swiftly, feel the crisp air against her face, let it 'blow the cobwebs away.' It was all over and she was a fool to let sentiment master her. It ought not to matter to her whether Richard Bromley went or stayed. These regretful, desolate feelings were against her creed of life.

When she reached Gale Towers and joined Vera and Tony down on the beach, she was mistress of herself again, and there were no traces of tears on her face. But she was a little white and grim. Tony took it for granted that she was missing Richard. He tucked an arm affectionately through hers as they marched along the sunlit beach to their favourite bathing-cave.

'Cheer up, Billie. Dick'll soon be back, won't he? It's a sell having to leave you on the honeymoon, and I expect you're thoroughly fed up.'

Her mouth twisted, but she answered the boy abruptly:

'Poof, no—no nonsense like that about me, my child!'

When Tony had disappeared into his own bathing-cave, and Billie was alone with her cousin, Vera attempted to discuss Richard.

'It'll be hopeless down here without him, and I can't think why you——'

'You'd do better not to *think* about Richard and me at all,

164

Vera,' said Billie sharply. 'He's gone, and I don't wish to talk about him.'

Vera crimsoned and jammed her blue rubber cap over her golden head with a savage little movement. She thought Billie a fool; Richard had been a fool ever to marry her, and a bigger one to have ignored her, Vera, and gone off in a huff this morning. She had done her best to comfort him, and all that had happened was that she, had been made to feel a fool! It was really very trying. However, Billie's sharp voice and grim face forbade further discussion of Richard. In silence the two girls proceeded to disrobe. It was a very quiet, depressed bathing party this morning.

Billie let Vera and Tony go into the water first. She sat huddled on a rock in the sunshine, slim arms hugging herself, eyes fixed moodily on the horizon. Mechanically she watched a steamship steam slowly along, leaving a thin trail of smoke behind it. But she was not thinking of the ship. She was thinking of Richard ... Richard in a stuffy third-class carriage on this hot, summer morning, journeying up to town ...

Just to the right of her lay the slab of seaweed-covered, glistening rock over which he had slipped and hurt his head. Only yesterday! But it seemed like an age. So much had happened between them since that accident.

She realised suddenly that she could never stay down here in Tintagel and lose herself in gloomy reflections. It was altogether unlike her, and would drive her crazy. She sprang from the ledge on which she had been poised and ran to the water's edge. After a quick swim and brisk rub down, she dressed and made her final decisions, which she announced to the others as they walked back to the house for lunch.

'I can't stay here and do nothing,' she said. 'I'm going up to town to-morrow, too.'

Vera gave her a curious look. Billie was really the strangest girl. What was wrong now? She had sent Richard away. Was she about to drag him back? Billie dispelled this idea by her next few words.

'I have an invitation from Lady Jo by last night's post, asking me to go to a dance she's holding this week-end. I shall accept it and stay at the Club, and come down here afterwards.'

Tony's violet-blue eyes gravely surveyed her.

'It sounds a good thing for you to do, old thing, but why stay at the Club? Why not with old Dick?'

She saw her mistake and flushed burning red.

'Oh—of course,' she stammered. 'He's going to some hotel, but hadn't decided which—was going to wire—we'll know to-night—then I—of course I'll join him.'

She was telling a deliberate lie to keep the boy in ignorance of the fact that she had parted from Richard for good. And she was amazed and shaken to find how sincerely she wished she was speaking the truth—that she was really going up to London to him!

CHAPTER 23

AFTER lunch she went straight up to her bedroom to pack. She intended to catch the early-morning train. Vera followed her, grousing.

'All very well leaving me down here with that boy, but it's going to be pretty dull.'

'Tony is a dear,' said Billie, pulling an armful of clothes out of a drawer and flinging them on her bed, 'only you have no idea how to treat boys of his age—you only know how to flirt with them when they're older.'

Vera glared at her.

'You're always nasty to me nowadays.'

'I'm sorry, but you do ask for it, V.—you're so silly. I'm really sorry, but my temper is not of the best at the moment,

166

and if you don't like being down here, go away, and I'll take the boy up to town with me.'

'Where could I go?'

'The bungalow, if you wish, but I don't want you in town with me. Quite frankly, you get on my nerves!'

Vera, crimson and sulky, hunched her shoulders.

'I don't want to go to the bungalow—it's lonelier than Gale Towers,' she said. 'I'll stay here with Tony.'

'All right.'

'But why are you dashing up to town?'

'Not, as Tony fondly imagines, to join Richard. I haven't the least idea where he is, and don't wish to know. If the wire comes, you can open it and hand it to Tony. I'd rather not know. I merely wish to get away and *do* things for a few days. I'm not in the mood for solitude.'

'I don't understand you, Billie.'

'I don't understand myself at the moment,' she said, with a short laugh.

'You seem very upset by Richard's going, and yet you could have kept him if you'd tried.'

'We're on the wrong subject again, Vera,' said Billie, in a dangerously quiet voice. 'That's why I can't bear you with me. I don't want to talk of him.'

'I believe you're in love with him all the time,' Vera dared to say.

Dead silence. Billie kept her face admirably free of expression, and took a suit-case out of a big cupboard.

'Ask Mrs. Massey to come here and help me pack,' she said calmly.

Vera marched out of the room.

'It would take a very clever person to understand Billie,' she muttered to herself as she went.

She was not to know that her shot had found its mark, that Billie's heart had given a great, sick throb as she had heard her cousin's accusation ... *'I believe you're in love with him all the time.'* ... But it was not true—it was not true—she was not in love with him, nor ever would be with any man. She

167

was only fleeing from this solitary, beautiful, romantic coast and from her own thoughts because her nerves were on edge and she had been upset by the quarrel with her husband. She regretted his friendship, his companionship—not the fact that she had rejected him as a lover. She did not want a lover. And she was *not* in love with him. Vera was a stupid little idiot—an interfering fool.

Tight-lipped, flushed, Billie picked up a pair of silk stockings, rolled them into a ball, and flung them viciously at the door to relieve her feelings. The door opened and the stockings hit Mrs. Massey full in the face, thereby causing that good woman a great deal of shocked surprise and hurt dignity. She was too well trained to do otherwise than stoop, pick them up, and hand them to Billie, her mouth pursed into a disapproving circle.

'I suppose you want these packed, madam?' she said.

Billie laughed weakly and took them.

'Thank you, Mrs. Massey,' she said. 'I'm terribly sorry they hit you. Yes, I want them packed. I'm going to town to-morrow.'

Mrs. Massey was not sorry. She had lived in a perpetual state of disapproval since the arrival of the strange 'young pair.' She said coldly:

'To join the master, I presume, madam?'

'Oh yes,' said Billie hastily.

She was not going to join her husband. It was the last thing in the world she intended to do. She wanted to get away from even the memory of him. She was going to plunge back into the old, gay, independent life with some of her old friends, and see how that worked. It would probably restore her mind to its former and proper balance.

But it struck her very forcibly even as she sat in the train that next morning, staring out at the scenery which flashed past her, that she could never be quite the same Billie again. She was still Mrs. Bromley—still wore a wedding-ring on her finger.

She wondered where Richard was and what he was doing.

The telegram containing his address had come, but she had ignored it—given it to Vera. That had been very silly, yet she had felt she would rather not know where to find him during the next few days. When she was more herself, she could communicate with him and make definite plans for the immediate future. But she had a queer, guilty little sensation in her heart. She had been left to take care of Tony, and she was deserting her post within twenty-four hours. That was not very brave or commendable of her.

'I can't help it,' she thought wretchedly, when the long, hot journey came to an end and she found herself in London. 'If I had stayed at the Towers I would have murdered Vera or driven the car to perdition, or something stupid. I must put Richard and this whole business right out of my mind!'

As she drove in a taxi to her Club in Dover Street, the hum and roar of London struck her like a great, noisy welcome. But she had never really liked London. It stifled her in the summer-time. Instinctively she thought of the house on the cliffs which she had just left, the glory of the sea and sky around it. She drove that picture from her mind and entered her Club, lips set, eyes bright with defiance. The vestibule was brilliantly lighted, soft carpeted, full of well-dressed women, and all very familiar to Billie, who had been a member of this Club for years. She never entered it without running up against an acquaintance. The first woman she encountered, just before she stepped into the lift, was Lady Jo, who generally played bridge or poker here until dinner-time.

Lady Jo fell upon Billie eagerly. Her face was paler, more haggard than ever; lips a startling shade of mauvish-red, matching the small felt hat on the black, Eton-shingled head. Immense diamond-drops hung sparkling from the exposed ears, the lobes of which were tinted to match her over-polished nails. Billie, who had not seen her for months, thought suddenly how revolting she was: a decadent creature of an hysterical era. But she had deliberately set herself out to plunge into the old, feverish, extravagant life into which she had been led in the past by acquaintances as rich and independent as herself, and shook Lady Jo's hand firmly.

'Hullo, old thing!' she said. 'You're the person I want. Let's have a beano of some kind to-night. I want cheering up.'

Lady Jo dragged Billy away from the lift to a small lounge, wherein she insisted upon ordering cocktails. She chattered like a magpie.

'Never dreamed I'd see you here, my dear old Billie!' she said, cigarette in the corner of her mauvish mouth, cocktail in one slender, aristocratic hand which was far from steady. 'Why aren't you in the country?'

'I've just come up from Cornwall. But why are you in town in the middle of the summer?'

'Because I adore London and can't keep away from it, my dear,' said Lady Jo, casting her long black lashes heavenwards. (She had had those eye-lashes sewn on at the cost of much pain and money, with satisfactory results.) 'The family are all up at the castle in Scotland, waiting for the glorious twelfth. But I couldn't bear the idea of lashions of aunts, uncles, and horrible little nephews from Eton; and mother who tells me twenty times a day that I'm a disgrace to the noble Earl, my papa. So here I am at the Club. Havin' a very good time, too. Bee Erskin's in town—so's Pat O'Sheeney and Lord Stranolger—Stranolger's a bore and an antiquity, but he has pots of cash; and Pat O'Sheeney's a darling—hasn't a bean but only his Irish eyes to commend him, so we've got a selection if we want a beano ... where's Vera ... why are you alone ... where's your husband? Heavens! I was forgetting you had one!'

Lady Jo had been talking breathlessly without ceasing— just one or two breaths for punctuation. But now she stopped and looked dramatically at the other girl.

'Your husband!' she repeated. 'Where is he?'

'Away on business,' said Billie calmly. 'That's why I'm here.'

'Are you sure you haven't quarrelled? Now, my dear, I warned you that men——'

'Please, Jo!' interrupted Billie, with a cold smile. 'Don't let's discuss my private affairs. I'm here to enjoy life, not to be lectured on the rottenness of man.'

Lady Jo drained her cocktail glass, shrugging her shoulders. Her haggard, feverish eyes rested on Billie with a suggestion of pity and 'I told you so.' She fully believed that Billie regretted her sudden marriage. But she refrained from questioning her further since she obviously was disinclined to talk. She wanted Billie badly at the moment. She was 'broke to the wide,' as she had reported to the 'noble Earl'; but that good gentleman, knowing his daughter, had refused further funds till the end of the month. He did not approve of the set in which Lady Josephine figured as a leader; of their wanton waste of money on horses, cards, and cocktails. Lady Jo could do with a 'beano,' herself, and Billie was generous. She ordered her another drink and suggested a dinner-party and a dance.

'I can take in several pals, and what about going to the Catkin Club? It's just opened, and a topping floor.'

'All right,' said Billie, in the mood to agree with anything. 'Some one was telling me about the Catkin the other day. Who do you know who is a member?'

'Bee Erskin ... she'll take us ... and I'm not sure old Stranolger isn't a member.'

Billie smiled a trifle ironically. She felt thousands and thousands of miles away from Tintagel and Gale Towers and the clean, sweet, simple life she had been leading with Richard and Tony and Vera. Stranolger, Bee Erskin, Pat O'Sheeney—the old hectic crew and Jo, the ringleader! Billie did not particularly like any of them. She rather disliked them. Yet once she had found them amusing, enjoyed throwing money away with them and on them. Why not do it again? Anything rather than remain alone, and mope. She had never moped in her life, and she was not going to do it now just because Richard had gone away. She had sent him away. Why mope about it? Where was he? What was he doing? ...

She snapped off the thread of her own reflections abruptly

and angrily. She did not want to think about Richard. She rose to her feet and took Lady Jo by the arm.

'Come on—I'm dirty and untidy, and I must get into some evening togs,' she said. 'I'll meet you later. You say when and where.'

'I'll dash round and get hold of the others and fix something. Phone you in half an hour,' said Lady Jo. 'Cheer-oh!'

She darted away through the vestibule. Billie walked thoughtfully to the lift.

That night Billie joined Lady Jo's hastily gathered party at the Kingfisher for dinner. She was none too pleased that Jo had chosen the Kingfisher. It reminded her of Richard—the one person she wished to forget. Here in the pretty blue-and-gold room she had sat with him before their marriage, making all their plans. Gloomily she stared at the table which they had occupied. It was also a coincidence that she should have put on the very same black lace frock she had worn that night, and the same flame-coloured velvet cloak.

Never in her life before had she been worried by memories, by this kind of discontented little ache at her heart. It infuriated her, yet she could not get rid of it. She tried to find distraction in the people with whom she was dining. Lady Jo was brilliant and amusing; Lord Stranolger hung over her, eye-glass in his eye, an inane smile on his withered lips, and seemed to Billie rather a disgusting old man who ought to be at home in slippers, reading his evening paper instead of aping the young man of 1927. Pat O'Sheeney, beside Billie, was an extremely good-looking boy with beguiling Irish blue eyes and a persuasive tongue. But Billie found him a bore and much too haggard and pallid. How could she help comparing him with Richard ... sun-browned, muscular, racing her over the sands, or through the radiant sea. Richard was a man—Patrick O'Sheeney was a 'poodle-faker' of the type that Richard would despise. Then Bee Erskin ... pretty, married, separated from her husband, spending twice her income ... what was there in Bee to satisfy the craving for real sympathy or decent, helpful friendship? Her charm was the froth on the champagne; the bloom on the grape; the gold-dust on the butterfly's wing—just as attractive and just as easily brushed away. Underneath she was a hard, scheming little person with an almost masculine capability for picking the right horse at a race-meeting, bluffing at poker, or buying and selling at the right price. When the charm of youth vanished, she would be a haggard, hard woman lacking in tenderness, in all the things a man expects to find in a woman.

Billie wondered what had come over her to-night. Why should she be so critical, so contemptuous of these people when she had, herself, followed in their footsteps, accepted their creed? Had her brief association with Richard Bromley altered her views—altered *her*?

She went on to the Catkin Club with her companions, laughing gaily with them, but conscious of an ever-deepening gloom and unrest. The Club was full of smart men and women, with a sprinkling of theatrical folk. The floor and band were first-rate, and the decorations artistic and rather beautiful. But even there Billie's spirits failed to rise. The atmosphere was stifling, and she found that she did not want to dance.

At midnight she had almost made up her mind to go back to her Club and retire to bed, when she noticed two newcomers, both men, walk across the dance-floor toward an unoccupied table close to Lady Jo's party. One was a tall fair man she did not know. But the other was only too familiar. She sat up straight and stared at him with a gasp of astonishment.

It was Richard . . . the old, bored Richard with cynical eyes and stern lips . . . hands in the pockets of his dinner-jacket, cigarette in his mouth. And now their eyes met and she saw him start, flush red, remove the cigarette hastily, and stare at her. Then, simultaneously, they advanced toward each other.

'Billie!' said Richard in a tone of amazement. 'What on earth are you doing here?'

'I might ask the same,' she said, with a weak laugh.

Her heart was beating much too fast for her own comfort and she knew her cheeks were scarlet. But to see Richard here, in the Catkin Club ... Richard who had occupied most of her thoughts despite her efforts to chase them away ... why, it was most disturbing! She was not sure whether she was terribly pleased or terribly annoyed at the unexpected meeting.

'I had no idea you were in town,' he was saying. 'When did you come up? This morning?'

'Yes. I got bored with Gale Towers.'

'I see.' He stared down at her, his own pulses on fire at the sight of her, the sound of her voice. All day he had been tramping round town to various offices where he was known, and wherein he hoped to find some kind of job ... and all day he had been thinking of his wife, picturing her down at the Towers, hungry for her, missing her, yet knowing that in all probability he would never live under the same roof with her again. It was equally a shock for him to see her. He was overwhelmingly glad.

'What a coincidence, Richard,' she said. 'What made you turn up at the Catkin?'

'That fellow with me—Roland Orme—is an old school-friend. We were at Marlborough together, and haven't met since the War. I ran across him in the city this morning, and he happens to be a member here and asked me to dine with him and come along. These sort of shows bore me, but I want a chat with Roland—he's a good sport—writes books and has made quite a success of it.'

'Of course. I know his name,' said Billie. 'How funny it all is. And I met Lady Jo Craigshaw at my Club, and she brought me here.'

Richard's eyes—bright, no longer tired and cynical—focused on the pary at Billie's table. His brows lifted a little.

'H'm. Rum-looking crowd, Billie.'

'I'm not sure you aren't right, Richard,' she said, with a half-shamed laugh. 'I'm sick of 'em, anyhow.'

'Come over to my table, then, and meet Roland.'

'I was just going home. But I'll come, of course. The others will be angry, but I've stood most of the drinks, so they can't object.'

With a curious little feeling of excitement she returned to her own table, leaving Richard to join his friend.

'If you'll excuse me, I'm going to the next table,' she said calmly, gathering up her cloak. 'That was my husband.'

'Oh, Gawd!' said Lady Jo, sticking her monocle in her eye and staring at Richard.

'Husbands always turn up at the wrong moment,' said Mrs. Erskin plaintively. 'Why don't you bring him over here? Doesn't he like the look of us?'

'I don't think he does,' said Billie frankly.

'Oh, I say, that's a bit thick,' complained Lord Stranolger.

'Billie, acushla, and is it that you're so married you've got to do what your husband wants?' asked Pat O'Sheeney.

'Oh no,' she said, smiling. 'I'm going to do what *I* want. 'Night, everybody!'

The party stared after the slim figure in the black lace gown ... watched her shake hands with the tall, fair-haired man, and then sit down between him and her husband.

'That's that,' said Lady Jo. 'Bill Carden always was a queer fish. Her husband's a good-looker, but a bit of a tyrant, what? I believe she's afraid of him. Oh well, let's dance. Come along. Thank Gawd I'm not married! I've always said matrimony ruins the best people. Poor Bill Carden's ruined ... not half so amusin' as she used to be.'

Meanwhile the 'ruined Billie' was enjoying her evening for the first time. Somehow being with Richard made her feel so much more 'at home' and at ease. Roland Orme was a delightful man, with a keen sense of humour and a ringing laugh. If he was surprised by this chance meeting with his old friend's second wife, he was much too well bred to show it. He thought her beautiful, in spite of the boyishly shingled head (he disliked the masculine cult of the modern girl), and wondered on what queer terms these two had married and parted again. Richard had only said a few brief words about

175

his second marriage when they had met this morning, and had hinted that it was not a success. Why not? Roland wondered. Mrs. Bromley ... Billie, as he called her ... seemed just the right kind of wife for Richard ... sensible, sun-browned, charming ... a more intelligent type than the silly woman who had run away from him.

With the writer's love of perception, of watching other people, Roland Orme watched these two ... his friend and his wife ... and wished by the end of the evening that he could see things come right between them. He had always been fond of Richard, and he liked Billie. Perhaps this unexpected meeting might bear fruit, he thought, and tactfully left them alone, when at two in the morning, they stood outside the Catkin Club waiting for a taxi.

'My digs are no distance from here—I shall walk, old man,' he said to Richard. 'You'd like to see your wife home, I'm sure. Good-night. See you as arranged in the morning. Good-night, Mrs. Bromley. I hope we shall meet again.'

He departed. Billie and Richard stood alone on the pavement under the starlit sky. And now an awkward silence fell between them. Neither had been prepared for this meeting; both were at a loss for words. Billie was the first to speak.

'Awfully nice man, that Roland Orme.'

'Topping fellow,' said Richard. 'Look here, Billie, jump into this taxi and I'll drive to your Club with you, then I can go on to my hotel.'

As they drove swiftly through the dark, deserted streets, another embarrassing silence was maintained until Richard, staring through the dusk at Billie's profile, felt the necessity to speak to her.

'It's so extraordinary, meeting you like this ...I—why it's ridiculous!' he said, with a short laugh. 'And you sit in that cloak with the chinchilla collar ... just like the night I took you out to the Kingfisher.'

'I know. We dined there to-night,' she said.

'Who on earth would think we'd been married and separated since then?'

176

'Your friend Roland must think us mad,' said Billie.

'So we are,' said Richard, with a grim smile.

'Oh well, anyhow, what are your plans?' said Billie, wishing that her heart would not race in such an absurd manner.

'I haven't any yet. I'm still looking for work.'

'It's ridiculous,' she began, 'my dear Richard——'

'No, Billie,' he interrupted gently. 'We'd better keep off any discussion. That's all over and done with. You know I've definitely decided to get a job, and Roland Orme's going to help me find something on one of the newspapers.'

'Oh,' she said, and subsided.

She stared out of the window. They were nearing Dover Street. And she realised not only that she was deadly tired but more depressed than she had ever been before in her whole life. Everything seemed wrong . . . upside down . . . life was wrong . . . a tangle—a beastly tangle which wretched human beings wove only too eagerly around themselves, and from which they were only too eager to extricate themselves.

She hated Lady Jo and her set . . . hated the thought of the old life alone. She dreaded saying good-bye to Richard again to-night . . . the prospect of an existence without him seemed to her suddenly, overwhelmingly unbearable.

He was unconscious of his wife's troubled thoughts. He was occupied fully with his own, which were much more devastating and wretched. The curious ache at Billie's heart was like the feeble stirring of a newborn thing. The hunger and misery of his was fierce and strong—the fully developed knowledge of passionate love. But he sat far apart from her, smoking, quiet, seemingly preoccupied. He dared not touch her, dared not speak one word of what lay in his heart lest there might be a repetition of the painful scene down at Gale Towers when he had lost self-control and swept her into his arms. Apparently he was forgiven for that. She had shown the old boyish friendliness and goodwill by leaving her friends at the Catkin Club to-night and coming over to his table—being charming to his friend. Better leave it at that . . . accept her generous friendship and cut out the wild, impossible dreams of teaching her to care in another way . . .

'Thanks for the unexpected pleasure of your company to-night, my dear,' he said lightly, without looking at her, when the taxi drew up before the Dover Street Club. 'I'll let you know what sort of luck I get with Roland to-morrow, and where I shall live.'

Her brow puckered.

'There's no reason why we shouldn't meet again quite soon, is there?' she said lamely.

'I shall be very busy. I've simply got to make some money, Billie,' he said abruptly.

The pucker between her brows deepened.

'Oh, money—I'm sick of the word!' she flashed.

'It will take me a considerable time to pay back Mr. Carden all that I have spent of his, all the same,' said Richard.

She looked up at him, her face hot and flushed in the dusk of the car.

'You know quite well I don't want you to pay it back just—just because of . . . what's happened . . . oh, it's absurd!' she broke off with a gesture of impatience.

'Don't let's argue the point, my dear,' he said. 'It's a pity that we must always argue when we are together.'

'Men don't understand women a bit!'

'You, my child, have never tried to understand men,' he said in a dry tone.

She stared at him, speechless. Her cheeks grew hotter. The reproach behind his words stung her. She told herself that he had no right to behave as though she had been the transgressor. She had married him under certain conditions and he had agreed to certain things which he—not she— had tried to alter. It was his fault that they had separated. Yet was it entirely his fault? Looking at it from his point of view, had she made it possible for him to keep his bargain, live with her as a friend? Was it his fault that he had fallen in love with her? She did not believe in love . . . yet it existed . . . there was no denying that fact, . . . and some fools thrived on it!

178

Billie's thoughts were jumbled and confused. She realised that she was altering fundamentally; that she was not nearly so prosaic, so hard-headed as she had been in the past before meeting Richard Bromley. Try as she would to force herself back into the old independent way of thinking and living, she found it difficult. She had grown used to Richard's companionship. She had relied on him—liked him. And now she was resenting their separation and the cause of it ... and that little ache at her heart was peculiarly insistent. She thought it was just loneliness and depression. She could not recognise the pain as love ... the birth-throes of that inevitable and mighty magnetism between man and woman which is primeval and which will last through eternity ...

'Oh well,' she said curtly, 'I'd better get out. Good-night, Richard.'

He was afraid even to take her hand. But as her pretty brown head turned from him he looked at it with hopeless yearning in his eyes.

'Good-night, Billie,' he said. 'How long will you be in town?'

'I have no idea. I thought I'd like it, but I find I don't,' she said, with a short laugh. 'I may get back to Tony and V. to-morrow. Anyhow—I'll let you know.'

'I want news of Tony,' he said almost wistfully. 'And later on, when it's cooler in town, I'd like the boy to live with me.'

She could not fail to realise from that how lonely he was feeling. She struggled with herself for a second in silence. Then with a shrug of the shoulders, and small mouth set, she said:

'Of course. We'll arrange that. Then I shall probably go abroad. 'Bye, Richard.'

'Good-bye,' he said.

She stood on the pavement, the flame-hued velvet cloak billowing in the night-breeze, a strand of brown hair across her eyes. That was his last view of her before she slammed the taxi-door, and with a harsh grind of brakes and gear, the vehicle moved on.

Then he sat back in the corner and covered his eyes with one hand.

'God!' he muttered. 'God ... to go on without her ... it'll be damnably hard! But what's the use of feeling it like this? ... She'll never care for any man ... it isn't in her ... she's a queer, sexless, maddening creature. But oh, God, I love her ... I love her more than I've ever loved any woman on earth!'

He felt that he had nothing, nobody to live for except Tony. And he would not have Tony for long. The boy was strong and normal again. Soon he would want to set forth and deal with his own life, make his own home; perhaps in time take a wife and settle down to domestic bliss.

Richard gave a bitter little laugh at the thought of his young brother marrying.

'I hope to God that he has better luck than I've had ... !' he mused.

CHAPTER 24

BILLIE, thoroughly out of temper with the world and herself, marched into her Club, prepared to seek her bed and forget her worries in sleep. She was yawning as she walked to the lift, and looked pale and heavy-eyed. It was just upon 3 a.m., and the evening, which had been boresome and exciting in turn, had robbed her of some of her magnificent vitality.

She was not destined to retire to her room in peace. The night-porter approached her with an orange envelope on his salver.

'Telegram came for you just after you went out, miss,' he said.

She took the wire and read it, frowning. But the frown gave place to an expression of dismay. The blood rushed to her cheeks, then receded again.

'Oh!' she said aloud, with a gasp. 'What a catastrophe!' She swung round to the weary porter.

'Get on the phone to the Regent Palace at once,' she said breathlessly, 'and ask for Mr. Bromley. He'll be just in by now.'

Then she read the wire again, her heart racing, her face pale with distress. It was from Vera, and ran like this:

'Come at once and tell Richard Regent Palace that Tony went walk alone this afternoon slipped down cliff seriously injured am distracted.—VERA.'

Five minutes later Billie was in the telephone-box talking to her husband. Her voice trembled.

'Yes ... it's awful, Richard ... I can quite imagine what happened ... Tony got fed up with Vera and went out alone. He's none to firm on his legs yet, and I suppose he tried to climb down the cliff-side near Trebarwith. It's all my fault; I ought to have stayed and looked after him.'

'No—it's my fault; I ought to have stayed with him,' came Richard's voice hoarsely. 'Billie, I hope to God the little fellow's all right. But Vera says "seriously injured."'

'Vera always panics—don't lose heart,' said Billie. 'But of course we must go down at once.'

'You'll come with me?'

'*Of course!*' she said almost angrily.

'Good for you. When can we go? How can we get there quickly? It's a quarter past three in the morning—hopeless——'

'There's quite an early train—about eight—to Camelford,' said Billie. 'I'll wire Rawlinson to meet us there in the car. It's no use attempting to go to bed. I couldn't sleep—could you?'

'Not a wink.'

'Very well, then, I'll come round to your hotel,' said Billie. 'We'll astonish everybody—at least, anybody who's up—by remaining in the lounge until seven, and then we'll have breakfast together.'

'I say, would you do that? It would be ripping of you,' came Richard's voice, none too steadily. 'You don't mind—your reputation and——'

'Reputation? Rubbish,' broke in Billie. 'Aren't we married?'

It was torment and delight to him to hear her say that, to realise that she recognised her marriage-tie. But just now he was full of the thought of his young brother. He loved the boy. To lose him, after all the effort of these last few months to get him fit and strong again, would be tragic. Vera had said 'serious injuries.' Richard was filled with apprehension.

Half an hour later, Billie was at his hotel. They had both changed from their evening clothes. She was in a tailor-made with a travelling coat and small black felt hat. She looked pale, but her eyes were bright and she no longer felt tired. She was fully awake, alive to the seriousness of the situation. She knew just what Richard was going through. She was, herself, extremely anxious, for she was fond of Tony. If the boy dies, it would be a calamity . . . a greater calamity for the brother who lived and who would be bereft of everything.

Richard had never known Billie in this mood. She astonished him by her gentle solicitude, her sweetness to him. He almost wished she would be her old, hard self . . . Her kindness nearly broke him down. But he managed to keep a stiff upper lip. They sat in the lounge and waited for the long hours to pass, smoking, talking, discussing all the possibilities of Tony's accident. Billie had sent off two telegrams—one to her cousin to tell her to wire for Sir Basil Graham if Tony were in the least danger, the other to her chauffeur ordering him to meet the first express from London, at Camelford Station.

They were trying, anxious hours, and both these people who cared for the boy, each in their own way, were nerve-racked and haggard by the time breakfast was served. They went out to watch the sunrise, feeling it impossible to remain the whole time in that deserted lounge. Billie never forgot that dawn. She walked at Richard's side as far as Charing Cross, and paused with him at Trafalgar Square, which was deserted and beautiful in the calm summer morning; the water in the great stone basin tinged to rose with the reflection of the flushed sky. She put a hand through his arm in a quiet, friendly way, and looked up at his haggard face.

'Courage, Richard,' she said. 'He may not be so bad as we think.'

He pressed her arm to his side.

'Thanks for your help, my dear,' he said. 'I couldn't have stood this night without you. You've been a wonder.'

'I've done nothing. I feel guilty somehow . . . as though the accident was my fault—I ought never to have left him,' she said, a lump in her throat.

'It's nobody's fault, really,' he said.

They were standing in the middle of the road, staring at the great, famous monument which had been erected to the everlasting glory of Nelson . . . their thoughts down at Gale Towers with Tony . . . both oblivious of their surroundings. They were nearly run over by an angry fruit-vender rolling his barrow from Covent Garden.

'Hi! Wot you doin' 'ere at five in the mornin', dreamin' in the middle of the road!' he yelled at them. 'Ain't you never seen Trafalgar Squa-are before?'

'Come, Richard,' said Billie, with a ghost of a smile. 'We'll have a lorry into us next. Let's walk back to the hotel and get a cup of tea.'

He yielded to the pressure of her arm, sighing. They walked slowly along the street toward the Haymarket. The sun rose higher; the rosy dawnlight faded and left a pure gleam of gold in the blue summer sky. Milk-carts and motor-vans rattled along the road, and the early workers of the great city emerged from their dwellings and began to scurry along the streets like so many busy ants darting out from a hill. The day had begun. London was awake. And both Richard and Billie were conscious of thankfulness. In a short time now they could set forth for the station and take their seats in the Cornish express. Once in the train they would feel well on their way to poor Tony. It would be a relief.

When they really were at last in the train, the journey seemed interminable. They talked very little. Richard was worried and 'distrait,' and Billie had that masculine asset of knowing how to express her sympathy by silence rather than words. When they did open up on the subject of Tony, she encouraged and soothed the man, who was inclined to be pessimistic.

'Honestly, Richard, I know V., and she is an alarmist of the first order. Don't cross your bridge till you come to it. I dare say Tony is all right,' she said toward the end of the journey.

He smiled faintly. Tired eyes rested on her with an expression of deep gratitude.

'You're a sensible little woman, Billie,' he said. 'You must forgive me. My nerves are all to bits.'

'Naturally,' she said. 'A wire like that is a beastly shock, and one never quite knows what lies behind it. But buck up, old thing, we're nearly there.'

They reached Camelford that afternoon. Rawlinson was waiting for them on the platform. He took the two suit-cases and they all walked out of the station to the waiting car. Billie, leaving her husband to give up the tickets, walked on ahead with her chauffeur.

'How is Mr. Tony, Rawlinson?' she asked.

'Very bad indeed, miss—madam,' said Rawlinson, who had been with Billie for two years and found it difficult to remember that she was no longer Miss Carden. 'It's a good thing Mr. Bromley has come down. I think it's only a question of time ...'

'Ssh,' said Billie, her heart giving a throb of fear for Richard. But he had heard. He joined his wife, his face grey, his mouth set in a grim line.

'So that's that,' Billie,' he said. 'Tony's dying.'

In the car, Rawlinson driving at reckless speed to Tintagel, Billie laid a hand on Richard's arm.

'Even now you mustn't give up hope,' she said. 'We can't be sure ...servants are always gloomy on these subjects, and it may be a rumour——'

He put one of his hands over hers, the muscle in his throat working.

'You're a dear,' he said, 'but it's no use stuffing me up with hopes. I haven't any left, anyhow. My only regret will be that I wasn't here with him . . .and I ought never to have left him.'

'It was for me to go away,' said Billie, trying to keep calm, although she felt like crying. 'It was my place to leave the Towers—not yours—and neither of us need have gone; but oh, what's the use of talking about that now?'

'No use,' said Richard, his hands locked between his knees. He stared at the beautiful rugged coast they were nearing, without seeing it. He was torn with anxiety and the desire to get to Tony before it was too late.

Vera met her cousin and Tony's brother at the door of the Towers. One look at her made Billie's heart sink. She knew Vera so well; she was an alarmist, but she never allowed other people's troubles to upset her unless she had good cause to be upset. She looked ghastly—and burst into hysterical sobbing the moment Billie greeted her.

'Oh, thank goodness you've come! It wasn't my fault, Billie . . . Richard . . . I swear it wasn't . . . he insisted on going out by himself . . . oh, I wish I'd never been left in charge!'

'Drop that, Vera, for Heaven's sake—we're all on edge—we can't stand melodrama,' said Billie, in the old hard way. 'Don't cry, please. Just tell us exactly what happened.'

Vera told them. Tony went for his walk yesterday after lunch, and did not come back. Later they—Mrs. Massey and Vera—went to look for him, found him at the bottom of the cliffs some quarter of a mile from home. He was a twisted, suffering wreck, but conscious, and had explained that he had tried to pick some samphire. Still weak on his legs, he had slipped, lost his balance, and fallen down on to the beach. It was not a very steep piece of cliff, but high enough to be dangerous. They had carried the boy home and sent for the local doctor at once. He had been doubtful that Tony would live, but on top of Billie's wire, they had telegraphed for Sir Basil Graham. The great surgeon had wired back that he would be down to Tintagel at once. He would arrive this evening.

'I hope to God he turns up in time,' Vera sobbed. 'Tony

looks pretty bad to me. Poor kid! He said what rotten luck it was, just as he was getting better and enjoying life again. Dr. Newcombe says he has broken the right leg and is suffering from shock and a good many cuts and bruises.'

'Well, none of that means he's going to die!' said Billie between her teeth. 'Richard——'

But Richard had gone. He had not waited for the hysterical Vera to complete her tale. He had rushed through the hall, passed old Trenance who gazed pityingly after him, and leaped up the stairs, three at a time.

Billie flung off her coat and hat, and followed.

They stood by Tony's bed, hearts palpitating with the grief and anxiety of it. A trained nurse from Tintagel, and Newcombe, the local M.D., were in the bedroom. Newcombe was of the old school; his methods were not up-to-date and he was of a melancholy and pessimistic temperament. He shook his grey head when Richard's anxious eyes questioned him, and shrugged his shoulders.

'I don't like the look of the lad,' he whispered.

But Billie—still with set teeth—defied the old man.

'He isn't going to die—I know he isn't. Graham will save him ...'

'If Sir Basil gets here in time,' said Newcombe gloomily.

Billie turned to Tony's bed.

The boy lay motionless, head bandaged, face pathetically young and delicate in the dim light of the sick-room from which the hot summer sunshine had been shut out by drawn blinds. Richard sat down and took one of the limp hands in his.

'Tony,' he said. 'Tony, old chap!'

For a moment Tony made no sign of recognition. Then he opened his eyes ... dark violet ... drugged. A drowsy smile passed across his face.

'Hullo ... Dick ...' he said.

'How are you, old man?'

'Sleepy,' came the slow answer. 'Rotten shame ... falling over ... like that ... Dick, I feel pretty queer ... can't see anything much ...'

186

'I expect that's the morphia they've given you, old chap,' said Richard. 'You'll be better soon.'

'Am I ... dying?'

'Of course you aren't,' said Billie, who was standing at the foot of the bed, and now her face was convulsed. 'Of *course* you aren't, you old duffer.'

'Is that ... Billie? Dick ...'

'Yes.'

'Tell me ... I'm worried ... Vera hinted ...'

'What, old man? Ask anything you like,' said Richard bending over him.

'You and Billie ... aren't separating ... are you?' panted Tony.

It was Billie who answered that question. In a flash she understood what was on the boy's mind. He was worrying because the stupid, senseless Vera had suggested that her cousin's marriage was not the success it seemed.

Deliberately she slid an arm around Richard's shoulder.

'Indeed, we aren't separating! Whoever heard such rot? V. was teasing you. Dick and I ... will never leave each other, Tony.'

Richard was not in the state of mind to attach any weight of importance to his wife's words, but instinctively he put an arm about her waist. A smile spread over Tony's white face.

'Good for you ...' he said. 'I'm glad. I can—sleep—now ...'

His eyes closed. Sudden terror shook Richard. He released Billie, and swung round to Newcombe.

'Doctor—come here,' he said hoarsely.

Newcombe put on his pince-nez and advanced to the bed, fingered the boy's pulse. A surprised look came over his melancholy old face.

'Ah-ha ... ahem ... much better pulse ... I declare the lad is sleeping normally.'

Richard stood up and squared his shoulders. He felt a relief too great for words. But Billie slid an arm through his, and dabbed fiercely at her eyes.

'I knew he wouldn't die, Richard ... buck up ... once Graham comes, all will be well ... you'll see.'

CHAPTER 25

MUCH later that same evening, Billie knocked at the door of Richard's bedroom. Sir Basil Graham had come, and was still with Tony and the nurse. The boy was out of danger, and the great Harley Street man had given them all fresh confidence. He would soon put the broken leg right. It was a question of time ... a set-back in Tony's splendid progress ... but he would get better ... be as right as ever he was.

The glad news seemed to have overwhelmed Richard. He had retired and locked himself in his own room since dusk. Now, in answer to Billie's knock, he opened the door and let her in.

He looked worn and tired, but he smiled at her.

'Sorry if I've been an idiot, Billie—but I had to be alone for a bit. The boy's all right?'

'Asleep and going along splendidly. Graham is still chatting to the nurse, giving her instructions. He's been a dear to us. He's staying at King Arthur's Castle Hotel for the night, and looking in on Tony in the morning.'

Richard gave her a searching look, and became suddenly aware that she was pale and shadowy-eyed.

'Oh, my dear girl, you must be tired out!' he said. 'No sleep last night ...and that long journey ...'

'Oh, I'm right as rain,' she said. 'Poor V.'s retired to bed in hysterics. But I'm terribly fit.'

'You're a wonder,' he said. 'And there aren't many wonders in the world. And thank you, my dear, for what you said to cheer poor old Tony up. I shall never forget your kindness.'

A wave of red darted across her cheeks. She dug her hands into her pockets. Her eyes dropped before his.

'Richard,' she said. 'I didn't say what I did to Tony just to cheer him up. I meant it.'

'No, of course not. We have arranged to separate.'

'Listen, Richard,' she said. 'Nothing will induce me to separate from you. First of all because I—I don't want to . . . secondly, because I don't intend that boy to get better and then find we have made a muck of things.'

He stared down at her, his own face growing hot, his heart leaping.

'You don't realise what you're saying, Billie.'

'Yes, I do,' she declared.

She came nearer him, nervously pulling at the tie she wore. Practical, unsentimental all her life, she found it exceedingly difficult to be otherwise even now. Yet she knew in her heart of hearts she wanted to be otherwise . . . that it was not merely out of pity for Richard, or consideration for Tony that she had changed. She felt new, stirring emotion which tugged at her very heart-strings and brought her to express her new-found womanhood despite herself. She said in a swift, low voice:

'Richard, I'm not going to argue with you. But I meant what I said in Tony's room.'

'That we—aren't going to separate?' he stammered.

'Yes. I'm going to be—your real wife, Richard.'

He looked at her with unbelieving eyes.

'My dear,' he said, 'this is rubbish—you're just being kind—generous——'

'I'm not. I've felt like this for . . . for a long time . . . I mean since you left Gale Towers to go and look for a job.'

Then she added in an almost angry tone:

'Richard, you're making it awfully hard for me, and you know I'm not used to it . . . you know . . .'

She broke off, and suddenly overcome by shyness, covered her burning face with her hands. He gave a low cry and caught her in his arms.

'Billie, Billie ... what are you trying to tell me? Do you honestly mean you've changed ... that you care a bit ... what becomes of me?'

She looked up at him, her eyes brilliant with tears.

'Of course I care. I've always liked you. Now I find I can't do without you. I've tried to make myself believe there's no such thing as love, but there *must* be ... oh, I'm hopeless at saying the right thing, but I swear I can't do without you, Richard!'

He said:

'Oh, Billie, Billie ... my wife!'

'A rotten sort of wife I've been up to now. But I'll try and make up for lost time ... Dick,' she said very softly.

He did not kiss her—could not even speak to her; tell her what she meant to him; how incredibly dear she was; how beloved from the cropped brown head to the slim feet ... he could only hold her close, close to his heart and press her cheek, wet with tears, against his own.

She put an arm about him very awkwardly, like a schoolboy, unaccustomed to demonstration, and secretly enjoying the caress.

Later still, that same fateful night, Billie found herself in a position which she would once have despised, but now admitted to be extraordinarily comforting—curled up in Richard's arms on the drawing-room sofa.

'Of course, darling,' he was saying, 'this doesn't make any difference to my intention to work. I can't be dependent on my wife, or her relations ...even under such changed and wonderful circumstances.'

'Oh, all right,' said Billie. 'It's no good arguing with you ever—you're so stubborn. Work if you must. But first of all I insist—at Uncle Silas's expense, mark you—upon being taken for a real honeymoon.'

He thrilled and caught her closer.

'This from you! I'm surprised, after all your theories upon love. What *is* love, may I ask?'

'That is an unanswerable question,' said Billie. 'And I don't intend to turn into a dutiful wife, and I refuse to be reminded daily of my theories upon love. I have none. I've given up the problem.'

'I don't know that I care,' said Richard thoughtfully.

'Still, I am inclined to agree with jolly old Shakespeare,' said Billie, '"'Tis not hereafter . . . present mirth hath present laughter . . ."'

'Oh, quite so!' said Richard. 'And that verse also includes the line "Then come kiss me, sweet and twenty . . ."'

She raised her lips to his and returned his kiss with a passion that amazed and enchanted him. But she was still the old Billie he adored. She drew away from him, cheeks burning, eyes aglow, and said in the boyish, sheepish way so dear and familiar:

'Oh, I say, Dick, we're being frightful fools! Give me a cigarette!'